ANGEL OF DEATH

AND SO IT BEGINS...

ANNA-MARIE MORGAN

ALSO BY ANNA-MARIE MORGAN

In the DI Giles Series:

Book 1 - Death Master

Book 2 - You Will Die

Book 3 - Total Wipeout

Book 4 - Deep Cut

Book 5 - The Pusher

Book 6 - Gone

Book 7 - Bone Dancer

Book 8 - Blood Lost

Book 9 - Angel of Death

Book 10 - Death in the Air

Book 11 - Death in the Mist

Book 12 - Death under Hypnosis

Book 13 - Fatal Turn

Book 14 - The Edinburgh Murders

Copyright © 2020 by Anna-Marie Morgan

All rights reserved.

No part of this book may be reproduced in any form or by any electronic or mechanical means, including information storage and retrieval systems, without written permission from the author, except for the use of brief quotations in a book review.

For my beta readers Jenny and Barbara. Thank you.

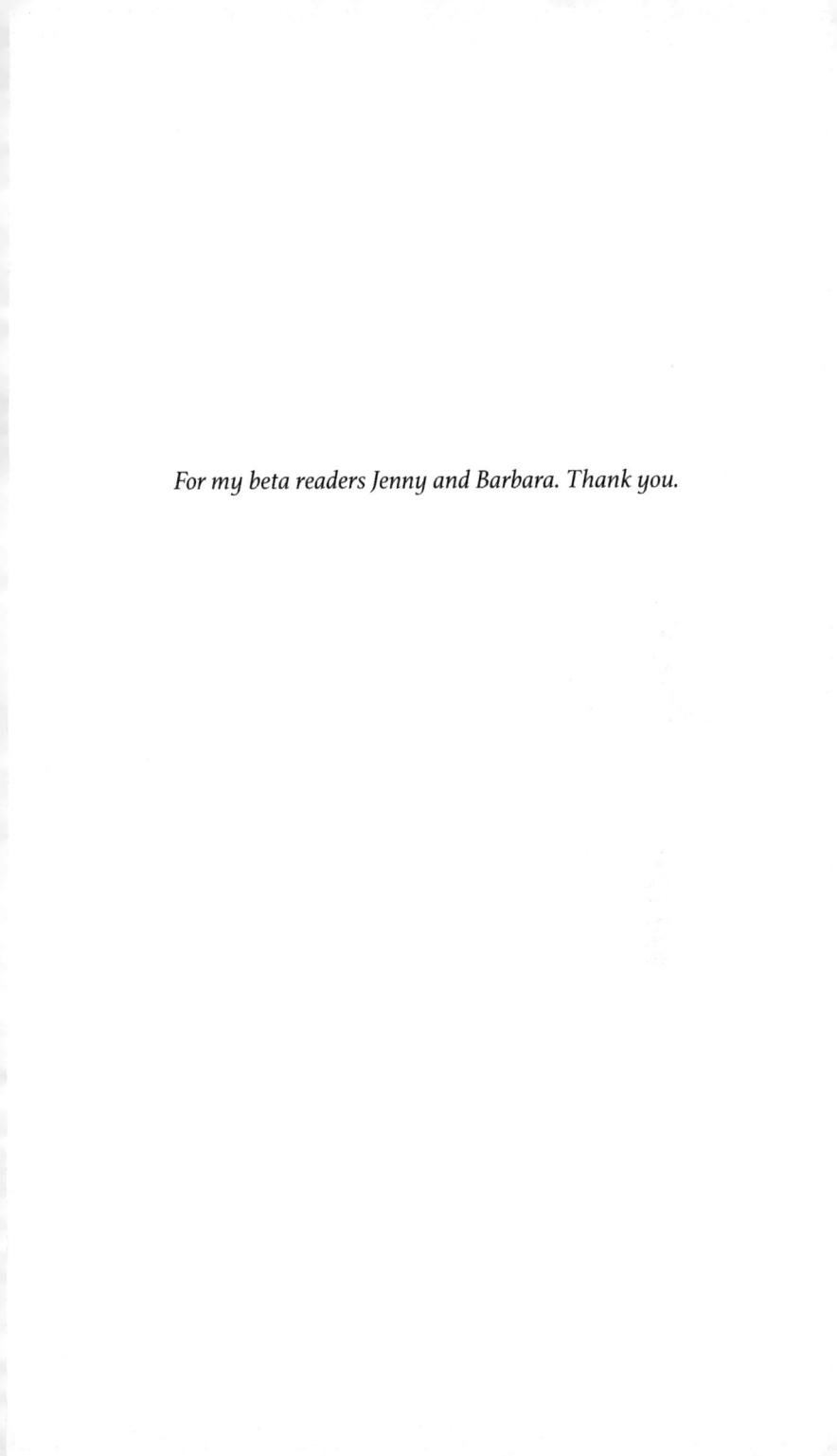

FOREWARD

I sit in the wood, my eyes closed
Inaction, no falsifying dream
Between my hooked head and hooked feet
Or in sleep rehearse perfect kills and eat.

∽

Excerpt from 'Hawk Roosting' by Ted Hughes.

1

ALONE IN THE WOOD

~

Krista crouched low, chin on her knees, hugging them tight as she listened to the throaty engine of a nearby truck. Holding her breath as though the vehicle itself might hear her, she pushed tangled hair from her face, telltale mud staining her cheeks. It wouldn't do to get caught. Not now. Not while she was on her own.

The truck continued on and she exhaled with a sigh, reaching into her pocket for the perfume bottle and the precious spray she had prepared that morning

The icy air had hints of moss and dank wood. It pervaded her clothing and would cling to her for the rest of the day. There was no regret in that. She was of the earth and to the earth she would return. At one with the environment.

With the sun not yet above the horizon, she worked with focussed efficiency, spraying foliage and gnarled tree roots along the path she knew the dogs would take. And they would come through here, yelping in excitement, striking fear in the hearts of the helpless. But now the canines would falter, blundering and falling over one another in their eagerness to kill. Sniffing and panting in confusion while searching for a scent much harder to find, hearing the hooves of approaching horses, their riders dressed in finery. These huntsmen had little patience with dogs not up to the job.

She stood to survey her work and ease the ache in muscles stiffened by the bone-chilling cold.

Krista swung her head at the crack of a twig behind her, just before the mallet crashed into the small of her back with a sickening thud. Excruciating spasms radiated from her core to every part of her.

It took barely a microsecond for her legs to fail, but it seemed a minute, maybe two, in a mind wracked with pain. Adrenaline surged through every artery, capillary and vein.

She lay on the ground, consciousness fading in and out. The mallet smashed her right arm followed by her left.

She didn't register the blow to the left.

He lifted her as a child might lift a doll. A dead weight. Limp and still. Broken limbs swaying in the air as he hoisted her over his shoulder and carried her to the back of the Land Rover. He threw her in like he might an old sack. There was no resistance. She landed in a misshapen heap.

The early January sun, barely above the horizon, encouraged the frozen dew to join the mist blanketing the valley below. All was quiet, save for the birds which darted to-and-fro, tossing up leaves to peck at the crawlies beneath.

He filled his lungs, feeling the sun heating the area between his shoulder blades, controlling the clouds he created with pursed lips as a smoker might when making smoke rings.

The mallet, he threw after the woman. Even if she were to regain consciousness, she couldn't use it. Not now.

He moved with purpose, yanking open the driver's door. The hunt would come past within the hour, finding her the way he wanted them to. On her very own stage. Her death scene.

∼

"Good Morning, ma'am." Callum cleared his throat, hands thrust deep in his overcoat pockets.

"Hello, Callum." She took in his sunken eyes, and lips pressed in a thin line, and felt a knot developing in her gut. "It's not good, is it?"

He shook his head, turning to approach the victim with her. "She's been dead for several hours, at least. Body's cold, but cooling would be relatively fast at this temperature. She wasn't here last night according to the gamekeeper."

"Is Hanson here?"

"He is." Callum jerked his head. "He and his team are setting up equipment in the tent."

They discarded their coats on boxes, at the edge of the cordon, grabbing SOCO suits from an open crate.

Yvonne took a deep breath, her eyes examining the trees and fields along the Kerry Ridgeway, on the edge of Ceri Forest, in a place known as Block Wood. In the distance, a thick, white mist rose in the valley below.

The victim was fully clothed and propped against an Ash tree surrounded by conifers, not two hundred feet from picnic tables and the main road.

Her killer had chosen a public place, situated atop a tourist site on a road used in ancient times by drovers taking their goods and cattle from Wales to the thriving markets in England.

The woman appeared as if she were sleeping, head lolled to the left. Dressed in a Khaki army surplus coat and black jeans, there were no visible marks on her from the front. He had splayed her legs and a single white Swan feather lay between them. Plum-coloured boots held clumps of mud and leaves, and shredded grass protruded from the toes.

Her eyes were wide open, frozen in a death stare indicative of the shock of the assault and a horror that was unexpected.

Her arms, pulled behind her and wrapped around the tree trunk, had bones protruding under, or even through, the skin. Long, dark hair lay in a plait over her shoulder. He had placed the girl's hands one over the other and driven a nail through them.

"Crucified." Callum sighed, his eyes, half-lidded, as Yvonne joined him behind the tree.

"She was conscious for a time." Hanson, the pathologist, approached from the tent. He pointed to the victims hands. "The flesh is torn around the nail as though she spent some time trying to pull herself free. She couldn't because her upper arms were shattered by the blows. I suspect he also broke her back. I can't confirm that until we get her into the morgue."

"So, he smashed her arms to make them wrap around the tree?" The DI rubbed her chin. "What's with the feather? Did the killer leave that there? It looks placed, to me."

Hanson nodded, moving his mask down from his mouth. "There's resin or glue present on the tip as though it had been a part of something else. I agree, it's a staged

Angel of Death

scene. As soon as the photographer has been, we'll bag it for testing. One thing's for sure, a bird didn't drop it here."

Yvonne knelt to peer at the thick substance on the feather. She pursed her lips. "I wonder how long she was conscious?"

Hanson shook his head, his expression, grim. "She likely died from a mixture of shock and cold and, likely, internal blood loss. At these temperatures, I don't think it would have been longer than two hours. I'll know more after the postmortem, I'll give you a better idea then. We'll do a full range of toxicology tests as well, as you'd expect."

"Who found her?"

Callum checked his notes. "Trevor Tindall, the gamekeeper for Ryde Hall reported it."

Yvonne made a note. "Thank you."

A large plastic spray bottle caught her attention. "What's in that?"

"I can smell citronella. Can't you?"

"Yes, you're right. Looks like she was a hunt saboteur."

"I'd say so."

Dewi approached from the road. "I just heard. Got here as fast as I could." He held his jaw. "Dental appointment. Sorry."

"Brace yourself, Dewi." Yvonne looked back towards the victim.

"Oh God." Dewi ran a hand through his hair, a look of recognition on his face.

"Dewi?"

"That's Krysta. Krysta Whyte."

"Known to us?"

"Yes."

"Hunt saboteur?"

"Yes, she and her friends have come to our attention

several times over the last few years. Land invasions, that sort of thing."

"She'd annoyed a few landowners then?" Yvonne pursed her lips. "A motive for the killing, right there. Callum, could you set up an interview with the owner and gamekeeper of Ryde Hall as soon as possible? Also, check out anyone else with reason to be on the land and in the forest."

"Will do, ma'am."

"And speak to uniform. I want this place gone through with a fine-tooth comb. We'll need formal identification. Dewi, we'll break the news to Krysta's parents."

Dewi blanched. "Right, you are."

2
ANGEL OF DEATH

He examined his wings, pupils widening, forehead lined above the eyes as he found a gap in the left one. That wouldn't do. He pulled it towards him, grabbing the plywood frame from the back, running his nose along the soft feathers at the front, breathing the bird scent.

On the stove, a steaming pot bubbled away, rabbit skins breaking down and releasing the collagen that would make his glue. Not long, now. His wings would be whole again.

Lifting the right one, he slid his arm through leather straps, made to hug the forearm and upper arm, like one might find on a shield. Likewise, the left.

Above his head, they cast a menacing shadow on the wall opposite, where he hovered like a black hawk, diving for prey, or else a demon, scrutinising potential victims below, while holding power over their life or death.

The surge of blood and adrenaline conjured up the feeling he could do anything. Be anything. Raw and omnipotent. Divine and monstrous.

Turning to the mirror, he examined himself, naked from

the waist up. The muscles of his torso, taut and undulating, he held the wings aloft once more. In his mind, he soared above the fields and houses, master of all, eyes wide for his next kill.

A hissing from behind, reminded him of the boiling pot. He checked his watch. Three hours. The stew would require at least another three hours before the remains turned to glue.

He grabbed a bottle from the shelf and poured olive oil into his palm, applying it to his shaved chest, using both hands to spread it around while studying his image in the mirror and caring not that his skin was pale or beginning to show the signs of age. He found pleasure in it. It would have pleased him even more if he could have been as white as the swan feathers comprising his wings.

Throwing himself to the floor, he began press-ups, alternating between full palms, knuckles, and thumb and first finger until, barely having broken a sweat, he counted fifty. Then, it was crunches of various sorts followed by a run, for which he drove himself to the lakes near Bwlch-y-Garreg. Middle of nowhere and stunning in its bare, windswept beauty. Green hills to the fore gave way to purple hills in the distance.

Lenticular clouds peppered the azure sky, reflected in the water below. Patterned ice lay thick among the reeds as his breath rose in a fine mist. The cold air hurt his lungs. He liked that. It tingled his skin and brought his thoughts into sharp focus.

He pushed himself hard. Five miles in fourteen-and-a-half minutes.

Sweat beading on the end of his nose, he stopped dead as he caught sight of a man in a flat cap, staring out over the lake, cane in one hand and a pipe in the other, spoiling the view. He imagined pushing him in, holding his head under until the bubbles ceased before watching the body sink into the cold, deep water.

"Nice day for it."

He started. The man with the pipe had turned to greet him and, though his mind was engaged in evil, he waved back.

Irritated by this involuntary reaction, he scowled and continued running, vest clinging to his skin. He would head home only after he was spent.

3

ED LAWTON

Ed Lawton stubbed his cigarette in a half-filled ashtray on the home-made coffee table between them. At least, Yvonne thought it home-made, fashioned as it was from a weathered wooden pallet. He turned his attention to rolling another smoke, frowning in concentration.

Yvonne watched in silence as he spread the tobacco along the middle of the paper. His dark head bent forward to lick and seal it.

Yvonne ran her hands down her wool-mix skirt. She cleared her throat and his eyes rose to meet hers, their cool-grey glistening from the tears he held onto.

"I'm sorry for your loss." The sentence clotted in her throat which she cleared while watching for movement in his face. "I'm aware that this isn't an easy time for you-"

"You're right. It's not." Ed rose from his chair and walked to the window, one hand combing through short, sandy hair. He stood with his back to her, his linen shirt and jeans, crumpled like he'd spent the night in them.

She chewed the inside of her cheek.

"We told her not to spray alone."

"Who's we? Who else understood that she sometimes went on her own?"

"Me and her other friends from our saboteur group."

"Could you give me a list of their names?"

"Sure." He walked back towards the DI.

"Why did she go there alone?"

"I don't know. I mean, I don't imagine what she was doing was all that effective, anyway. But she thought it helped. She would always join the rest of us later, but she'd start alone, at the crack of dawn, spraying the places the foxes might go to ground before meeting with us for more general disruption and monitoring of the hunt."

"When you say monitoring-"

"Filming. We film many of the hunts we follow."

"Do you have any recent films with Krysta on them?"

"We do. Most of them are on our Facebook page, including one or two in which someone assaulted her."

"I see. I would like to see those. Would you write down the name of your page for me and the names of your friends?" She handed him her notebook and pen.

"Sure. I'll give you the name of our main page, you'll find all of our saboteur colleagues and friends on that page." Ed scribbled it in her book and handed it back to her.

"Thank you. How long had Krysta been a saboteur?"

"She was one of our longest serving members. Started a few years before I did. She began with her local group at college around ten years ago and, when I met her, she told me it had been the first student society she joined as a fresher."

"Is that how you two met?"

"No. I didn't meet her until two years ago. I was with the North Wales Hunt Saboteurs and we met up with the

Shropshire guys to disrupt a Shropshire hunt. We regularly work jointly these days. She stood out. She was so... so committed. Determined. I admired her for that."

"How long were you living together?"

He spun to face her. "You know, she would have found all this attention from police ironic. She spent years trying to get your lot to help enforce the law and stop illegal hunting. She felt the responses she got were wishy-washy and half-hearted. Her words. She didn't believe the police cared about the ban. And, now, here you are, investigating her murder, which happened while she was trying to do your job for you."

"My job is to investigate murder." Yvonne kept her tone even.

"Yeah, because humans matter more than animals, right?"

"I didn't say that."

"But them's the rules." He sneered at her.

"I don't make the rules, Ed. I just work within them, doing what I can. You want Krysta's murder solved, and the perpetrator put away, don't you?" She tilted her head as though to peer under his half-lidded eyes.

"Of course I do." His lips moved, but his teeth didn't. They remained clenched, his expression broody.

He rolled up his sleeves, and the DI spotted the many freckles amongst the hair on his arms. "Where were you on the morning Krysta was killed?"

"I was here, waiting for her to rejoin me before we set off to Ryde Hall farm in the vehicles. When she didn't show, I assumed she'd gone straight there, and I travelled alone. I was late to the hunt that day, but the other monitors can confirm my arrival."

"What about while you waited for her? Can anyone corroborate your presence here?"

Ed shook his head. "I don't think so."

He sighed. "Krysta would have sacrificed her life to save a fox or any animal. That's the sort of person she was. Seems, she did just that. I don't expect you to understand." His eyes narrowed, face muscles twitching.

The DI saw the clenched fists and realised a fiery temper lurked within the young man in front of her.

Her voice was soft. "I still need to do my job. Krysta deserves nothing less."

"Did she suffer?" Ed searched her face.

Yvonne took a deep breath, unsure of what to say. If he was innocent, she did not want to cause him further pain.

"She did, didn't she? Your silence says it all."

"I can't give you specific details at this stage, Ed."

"Right."

"We will need your finger prints and all of your pairs of boots, I'm afraid. A forensics team will want to go through your place and carry out tests."

"For blood?"

"Among other things."

"So, I am a suspect."

"Anything else to tell me?"

He shook his head.

The DI pursed her lips. "I am sorry for your loss. I won't rest until we catch Krysta's killer, Ed."

He nodded, his eyes on the floor between them. "She deserves justice."

"I know."

4

BROKEN

The lights in the morgue were blinding after the shadowy streets outside.

Roger Hanson pulled on a clean pair of latex gloves, his forehead furrowed in concentration, his glasses half-way down his nose.

Yvonne shifted her weight between her feet and glanced at Dewi as he leaned against the wall near the entrance, notebook at the ready.

The pathologist manoeuvred the victim, his motion, matter-of-fact. "The killer attacked her from behind, she had no chance to react. He severed her spinal cord with the first blow. It landed between the 9th and 10th thoracic vertebrae." He pointed to the spot. "She wouldn't have seen it coming. The injury pattern suggests the instrument was most likely a long-handled mallet. Heavy."

"Ouch." Dewi grimaced.

"Quite... She would have collapsed, at which point the killer smashed the mallet down on her upper arms. I can't say what order, but he broke both humorous bones consistent with him hitting her whilst she lay against a firm surface, in this case the ground. He had rendered her immobile and she would likely have been unconscious, by that time, due to severe pain and the trauma of the assault."

"Broken whilst she lay helpless." Yvonne's gaze locked onto the bruised and misshapen arms and the holes in Krysta's hands, punctured and torn by the large masonry nail the killer used.

"Her killer likely enjoyed what he was doing. He wasn't squeamish."

Yvonne's eyes travelled to Krysta's head. Hair had fallen loose from Krysta's plait. It stuck to her head and neck with the sweat, exuded whilst she was nailed to the tree. Besides her wide-open eyes, it had been the only indicator of the pain and fear in her last moments alive. Her mouth lay open. Above her lop-sided jaw, a trickle of blood from her nose had dried on her upper lip. Yvonne was sure Krysta battled to live until the very last second.

The DI gritted her teeth, even more determined to catch whoever had stolen that life. She swallowed and cleared her throat. "How long was she alive on the tree?"

"An hour or two, but no longer than that. It fell below freezing again last night. In the height of summer, she might have survived until we found her."

"So, shock didn't kill her?"

"No. A contributing factor, perhaps, but it was the cold that got to her. Early results show there were no drugs or alcohol in her system."

"It's odd." Yvonne grimaced. "I swear I can still smell citronella. I guess it is psychosomatic."

"No, it is citronella." Hanson confirmed. "There were traces on her clothing, suggesting she spilled some on herself either in the preparation, or when spraying in the forest. There was enough that it penetrated through to her abdomen. That is what your keen nose is detecting, Yvonne."

"What about the feather, Roger? Did you hear from the lab about the substance on the shaft?"

"I did." Hanson rubbed his ear. "And it is a very interesting result. The substance is rabbit glue and, from its constituents, they think it is likely homemade. Few people make it at home, these days. It takes a lot of boiling of animal tissue and takes several hours and a lot of patience. It's not something someone would do lightly."

"Good result." Yvonne pursed her lips.

"I thought it might help you narrow down your killer."

The DI nodded, turning to gather her things. "If you find anything else which you think I should know, prior to the full report coming out, can you give me a bell?"

"I will, Yvonne." Hanson nodded, before turning his attention back to the victim on his table.

CALLUM TOOK the A4-size photos of the scene from under his arm. The file's absence revealed a damp patch in his shirt. He had left after everyone else the previous night.

"Thanks, Callum. How is the little one?"

"Caleb? Growing fast. He's doing well in the nursery, now that Sian has gone back to work for three days a week. Doesn't stop chattering. He's got his own little language."

Yvonne smiled. "It's a lovely age. My niece and nephew left that stage behind, but I remember it well."

"Do you think you might, one day...?" His voice trailed away.

The DI shook her head, a wistful smile on her face. "The likelihood of that is slim-to-none, now I've hit my forties."

Callum pursed his lips. "Women in their forties get pregnant, don't they?"

The DI turned her attention back to the photos.

Callum cleared his throat. "We found boot prints close to the body with a thick tread and we should name a manufacturer, later today. We didn't get specific tyre tracks, I'm afraid, ma'am. Too many vehicles coming and going. We have photographs of all the tracks we found. Might prove useful."

Yvonne spread the photos around the desk, pausing at the more graphic. "This was going further than killing her. This was some sort of punishment. Revenge, perhaps. Maybe, a warning to others? Come here causing trouble and this will happen to you."

She pointed to the close-up of Krysta's body with its head lolling to the side. "I can imagine the hopelessness she must have felt, Callum."

"Doesn't do to dwell, ma'am. We can't help her like that."

Yvonne sighed. "I know."

Callum tilted his head to study her face as she leaned over the desk. "Are you okay?"

"Yes." She straightened and placed her hands on her hips. "And, what's with the swan feather? It seems to be a calling card, but what is the significance?"

The DC tapped his pen against his chin. "I saw a thing on Facebook. Well, actually, my wife pointed it out to me. It was talking about feathers symbolising a visit from a guardian angel." He shrugged, and the colour deepened in his cheeks as though the revelation embarrassed him.

"Well, whoever left this was as far from a guardian angel as you could possibly get."

Callum nodded. "More like an angel of death."

"Mm. Angel of Death. I think you might just have named our killer, Callum. It could stick."

5

HEART-TO-HEART

"He may have been having an affair." Callum tossed his notes down onto Yvonne's desk and tucked a crumpled piece of his shirt back into his trousers.

"Who was having an affair?" The DI picked up the paperwork.

"Oh, sorry, Ed Lawton. An anonymous female gave us the tip. Claimed she is a fellow sab, but doesn't want to go on the record and wouldn't give us her name."

"I see..."

"She said she wasn't certain whether Krysta knew anything about the affair, but said that Ed had been seeing someone called Eva Wilde, from Shrewsbury, for about a year."

"A year? Wow. Do we know anything about Eva Wilde? We'll need a little more before we go asking Lawton about her."

"Got a few bits from PNC and from the desk sergeant, downstairs." Callum nodded towards the paperwork. "It's in there. Wilde is an environmental campaigner. She annoyed the council planning department a few years ago, campaigning against the bypass. Got herself arrested on three occasions for public order offences. She's also campaigned against the siting of wind turbines near the village of Abermule and has gotten her teeth into the proposed giant recycling plant near Welshpool."

"You say the affair was going on for a year?" Yvonne ran her hand through her fair hair, which had grown two inches past her shoulders. She regretted not having worn it up that morning, as it fell into her face again. "If it was going on that long, I'll bet Krysta found out about it."

Callum shrugged. "I agree, it would be hard to hide it for that length of time."

"And the anonymous caller refused to give her name?"

"She did, which seems odd, unless she thinks Ed killed his girlfriend and will kill her as well if he finds out she talked?"

"Or, perhaps, the caller was Eva, herself?"

"Hmm. Shall we go speak to Ed?"

"Not yet. Put a tail on him. If we talk to him now, he could deny it and tip Eva off. If we can evidence the affair, we'll have more leverage when we speak to him again."

"Right you are, ma'am."

"Someone we need speak to, ASAP, is the landowner near Block Wood. Emmanuel Tunicliffe. Krysta was convicted twice for harassing him and there was an injunction forbidding her from going onto his property. There was a great deal of bad blood between them. If she was hanging about on his land again, he may have lost his temper with her. Someone broke her back with a mallet. He could have done that in a fit of rage and then staged the crucifixion to throw us off the scent."

Callum nodded. "I'll arrange the interview, ma'am. I take it this will be a formal interview?"

Yvonne nodded. "Here, at the station and under oath."

"Understood."

∽

THE SEA ROLLED IN, crashing into the rocks and breaking into a fine foam which fizzed up and down the beach, turning it to a mass of froth as it receded.

It was the weekend, and Yvonne had met Tasha for lunch and shopping at the retail park in Aberystwyth. She had not been clothes shopping for some time and was badly in need of shoes, in particular. They finished the day with a stroll along the sea.

She stood atop a rocky outcrop, watching the water in silence, shirtsleeves rolled up in the early April sunshine.

"What are you thinking?" Tasha asked, reaching out a hand to steady the DI as she wobbled and appeared about to fall off.

"That days like these are precious in a world gone mad."

The psychologist frowned, her hand still on Yvonne's arm. "I try not to watch the news some days. It's depressing."

"Perhaps, there is something in the water." The DI gave a wry smile.

"Don't joke about it, lady. You could be right. We are all being poisoned with madness." Tasha took a step back. "Anyway, I hear you've been dating the DCI..."

"Wow." Yvonne grimaced. "News travels fast."

"It does in police circles." Tasha shifted her gaze to the ocean.

"Well, it wasn't dating. It was one time. One date. Not even a date. He invited me around for dinner."

"And?" The psychologist turned to face her, her head tilted, eyes narrow.

Yvonne's own eyes settled on Tasha's pale-blue cotton shirt. "He's a nice man."

"Nice..."

"Yeah, well, he's polite, charming and warm and he has a sense of humour."

Tasha stared at her.

The DI continued. "He has a beautiful home, well-kept. He's a good catch."

"I see..." The psychologist made semi circles in the sand with the bottoms of her walking boots.

Yvonne pursed her lips. "Aside from nerves at having dinner with a superior officer, I felt nothing."

Tasha's eyes flicked up to meet hers. "At all?"

The DI thought she detected a breathlessness in her friend's voice. "Nothing, at all," she affirmed. "I guess I should have done, shouldn't I? I mean, with all that going on for him." She jumped down from the rock. "But I didn't."

The two of them strolled along the beach in silence for several minutes, until Tasha interjected.

"So, is that it? Or will you see him again, to decide whether you feel any differently?"

Yvonne jutted out her chin, eyes blazing. "I won't."

The psychologist tried analysing the DI's expression, but Yvonne looked away and Tasha nodded, the muscles in her face stiffening as she suppressed the urge to smile.

The DI took a deep breath. "Anyway, heads back in the case, what might we be dealing with? I mean, on the surface, we've got an arrogant landowner with good reason to want Krysta off his case as our main suspect. But who nails a girl to a tree, whilst she is still alive and in considerable pain.

That's more than silencing, isn't it? Perhaps, even more than revenge? It's psychopathic."

Tasha pursed her lips. "Unless your suspect wanted to throw you off the scent and direct suspicion away from himself by persuading you to look elsewhere."

"Hmm... Are you telling me that a non-psychopathic personality could commit a crime like this?"

"If they were desperate enough, it's possible. You shouldn't rule it out."

"Understood. Hey, shall we move further around?" Yvonne referred to the bottom of constitution Hill, the famous promontory at the seaside town of Aberystwyth. They were on the stony beach at its base.

"We should be careful." Tasha pulled a face. "The tide is coming in. We don't want to get caught. People get cut off here."

"Yeah, you're right."

6

EMMANUEL TUNICLIFFE

"Dewi, grab your jacket." Yvonne called from the office doorway.

"Where we off to? And in such a hurry?" Dewi frowned.

"We're going to Ryde Hall. Home of Emmanuel Tunicliffe."

"Wait, isn't he-?"

"The landowner who was at loggerheads with Krysta Whyte? The one who requested an injunction against her? Yes."

"Got you." Dewi pulled a face. "Can we grab a sandwich? It's been ages since breakfast."

Yvonne grinned. "You and your stomach. Yes, Sergeant, we can pick up food on the way."

"Great. I'll get my tablet and catch up with what we have on him."

"No need, I have mine. He's thirty-seven, unmarried, and was an only child. He inherited his property and wealth from his father, Declan Tunicliffe, now deceased. Krysta Whyte harassed him over illegal fox hunting and the court sentenced her to an exclusion order with a five-mile radius around his home. She had been to his house many times to argue with him about the hunts."

"Tunicliffe denied illegal hunting, and was never prosecuted for it."

"Wait, wasn't Krysta's body found within that five-mile exclusion zone?"

"It was, Dewi, and Tunicliffe has been out of the country for a week, holidaying on the Southern coast of France. He caught a flight back last night. I want to speak to him before he gets the chance to settle down. Rattle him and see what falls out."

"Right. Let's do it."

As they passed through reception, the DI leaned on the desk. "Hey, Mike, can we have the keys to the shiny new four-by-four? We may need to go cross-country."

Mike narrowed his eyes. "It's pristine. Unscathed..."

"What? What do you think we will do with it?" Yvonne grinned. "Anyway, its not going to stay pristine forever."

Mike pursed his lips, a broad smile creeping across his face. "You can have it, Yvonne, but only because it's you." He looked across at Dewi. "Don't give the keys to him."

"Nice..." Dewi feigned a look of hurt. "That's the last time I buy you a pint, Mike Griffiths. And you're off my Christmas list."

"Christmas list? I was never on it." Mike laughed.

"Enough banter, boys, we've got a job to do." Yvonne grinned as she pushed open the station door.

~

YVONNE RANG the door bell next to the heavy oak doors of the porticoed Ryde Hall. A stocky man in his forties opened the door, wearing a wax jacket and looking as though he was about to leave.

"Can I help you?" He asked, placing a hand on his hip.

"Hello, I'm DI Yvonne Giles and this is DS Dewi Hughes. We are here to speak to Mr Tunicliffe. Is he about?"

The gentleman frowned and said, in a strong North-Wales accent, "I'm Trevor Tindall, Ryde Hall's gamekeeper. Mr Tunicliffe is out driving around the estate checking for fallen trees. The winds gusted at eighty miles per hour in last night's storm. He's out looking for any damage."

"What, he's doing that himself?" Yvonne tilted her head, narrowing her eyes.

"He's hands on, DI Giles. Likes to get stuck in." Tindall adjusted the tweed cap on his greying, dark hair. "I've got birds to check on. We've got a problem with our pheasants getting killed on the roads around here."

"I see. Well, I hope you round them all up safely. Do you know where on the estate we could find Mr Tunicliffe?" She stepped back from the door to allow Tindall to pass.

"He's probably close to Kerry village by now. He left over an hour ago. If I were you, I'd head over that way. He's driving a blue Land Rover."

~

Fifteen minutes later, they were half a mile from Kerry, and could see a blue Land Rover in a field below the road they were navigating.

"Want to go cross-country?"

Yvonne grinned at her sergeant's wicked expression. "Griffiths won't be happy about it."

"I know."

"Let's do it."

Angel of Death

They turned into the field of rough pasture, dotted with cowpats and orange-brown puddles of urine.

Tunicliffe's vehicle was already heading into the next field.

"What's he doing?" Dewi pressed harder on the accelerator. "There aren't any trees here."

"Perhaps, he's checking on the animals? Or, maybe, looking for something?" Yvonne's gaze moved from the Land Rover to the surroundings. "I'm amazed, he hasn't seen us yet."

"Or, if he has seen us, he doesn't want to talk." Dewi sighed. "We might have to give him a quick burst of the siren."

The DI shook her head. "We don't want to startle the animals. Use the lights."

Dewi nodded and flicked the switch.

"What on earth is he doing?" Dewi asked, again, when Tunicliffe continued despite their lights.

"Go on then, give him a quick burst of the siren." Yvonne frowned.

Beeeooop

The Land Rover showed no sign of slowing down, but neither did it speed up.

Beeeeooop Beep

"Okay, there we go." Dewi waved a hand at the windscreen. "Finally."

∽

Tunicliffe stayed in his vehicle, windows shut tight.

Dewi tutted and rapped his knuckles against the driver's side.

The DI stood behind her DS, near the police four-by-four, in case Tunicliffe took off again.

Just when they believed he would not open his window, it whirred down to half-way.

"Can I help you officers?" He uttered the question in a posh English accent.

Yvonne walked forward, resisting the temptation to ape the plummy voice.

"Mr Emmanuel Tunicliffe?"

"Yes... What is this about?"

"We'd like to have a word, if we might?"

"Well, I can't. I'm busy, right now."

"So are we." Yvonne gave a smile which didn't reach her eyes. "We still want a word with you."

"If you'd like to get out of your vehicle?" Dewi opened Tunicliffe's driver door.

"What is this? You can't just stop someone for no reason and this is private land." Tunicliffe stepped out.

Yvonne estimated him to be around six feet in height and in his early forties. His stubble-covered jaw wasn't straight. Twisted to the left, it gave him an odd appearance. "Have you not seen the news?"

"No." The word sprung from between clenched teeth.

"Someone murdered a woman on your land. Someone who we believe you knew."

Yvonne searched Tunicliffe's face and had the distinct feeling he recognised what, and who, they were talking about.

His facial muscles tightened as though he were about to say something, but decided against opening his mouth.

"Mr Tunicliffe, do you remember a young woman by the name of Krysta Whyte?"

"Oh, for God's sake..." Tunicliffe tutted, hands on hips,

spitting the words as he tossed his head back. "What's she been up to now?"

"Someone murdered her." The DI delivered the words cold, her eyes waiting for his reaction.

"Well, I'm not sup-" Tunicliffe stopped himself from finishing the sentence. He sighed. "She got enough people's backs up, meddling in other people's affairs. That girl couldn't leave well alone."

"What do you mean?" Dewi asked.

"Well, invading people's land, stopping them going about their legitimate business. Sticking her nose in where it was neither wanted nor needed. Enough for you?" Tunicliffe folded his arms while glaring at them, his Barbour jacket, tight across his shoulders. "What happened to her, anyway?"

"We're not revealing too many details, yet. However, we need to know where you were on Saturday morning? I must warn you that DS Hughes is wearing a body camera."

"What time?"

"Early morning, around six o'clock."

"In bed. Asleep."

"Really?" Dewi pulled a face. "Aren't farmers up at the crack of dawn?"

Tunicliffe sneered at him. "I'm not a farmer. And, anyway, I don't keep dogs to bark myself."

"Meaning, you have someone else who does the early work?"

"My gamekeeper."

Yvonne cleared her throat. "Weren't you involved in a fox hunt that morning?"

"It wasn't a fox hunt. It was a trail hunt, and I didn't set out until just after eight." He appeared pleased with himself, a smile flitting across his features. "You want to prosecute me? You really must invent a better excuse than that."

Yvonne rubbed her chin, her gaze thoughtful. "We will examine your alibi in fine detail, Mr Tunicliffe."

"I can't wait." His tone oozed sarcasm, his eyes challenging her to go up against him.

He thought this a game, she could tell, and she resented him for it. Yvonne pursed her lips and glared. Something about him got to her. Yes, her dislike was visceral. He had put himself near the top of her suspect list.

7
THE GAMEKEEPER

It took a while to find the gamekeeper's cottage. The woodland path stopped short, a muddy track leading from it to the home. Yvonne guessed it had once had comprised stones, now lost to time.

Dewi wore wellingtons. Yvonne looked at her flat shoes, caked in mud and leaves, and wished she had been as prepared as her DS. She attempted to clean them by scraping them on the large root of an oak tree.

The cottage looked as forgotten as the track, in need of repair or, perhaps, serious renovation. Remnants of cracked paint clung to the tiny window frames. Someone had broken a pane and taped a piece of plastic over the gap. Several tiles were missing from the roof and a large hole in the eaves provided nesting for local bird life.

Dewi knocked on the door, finding it ajar an inch. "Hello? Mr Tindall?"

He appeared from the back of the house, shovel in hand and red-faced, as though he had been exerting himself. "Go on in," he called to them, leaning the shovel against the wall and stopping to remove his boots.

Yvonne watched him do this and decided that she should also remove her shoes. Dewi wiped his boots on the sisal doormat.

"That was a bad business," Tindall said with a soft Welsh lilt as he filled the kettle from the tap.

"Do you live here alone, Mr Tindall?" Yvonne asked, casting her eyes around Tindall's tiny home. "Would you prefer me to call you Mr Tindall or Trevor?"

"Trevor's fine." He lit the gas under the kettle with a match, which he shook to kill the flame, before tossing it into the bin. "I live alone, yes."

"How long have you been here?"

"About twenty years."

"Did you never marry?" The DI tilted her head.

"I married a lass years ago, but she left. She said country life didn't suit her."

Yvonne wondered whether it had been the country life or the broken cottage which had sounded the death knell on their relationship.

"You said you thought it a bad business. Did you ever meet Krysta Whyte, Trevor?"

"I did."

Yvonne shot Dewi a glance. "How did you meet her? Through the hunt protests she took part in, or something else?"

"I bumped into her from time-to-time, including when she clashed with the boss, but that wasn't how I came to know her. We were relations. She was my sister's husband's daughter. A niece-in-law, if you like. Miles, that's my sister Kate's husband, had Krysta from his first marriage. His first wife died when Krysta was only three. Kate is his second wife. She loved the little girl and raised her like her own child."

"Sorry, I didn't realise you were related. I'm so sorry for your loss." Yvonne shifted in her seat. "Her death must have been a shock."

Tindall shrugged. "It surprised me, but I would be a liar if I said I knew her well. I chatted to her a few times, when she was down here, but it was general chit-chat. I wouldn't say anything to Mr Tunicliffe about her, though. There was bad blood between them. He couldn't stand her being on his land. Or any of them, come to that. Well, I suppose having an almost constant invasion would anger most people, when it is outsiders accusing you of illegal fox hunting."

"And was he?"

"Was he what?" Tindall frowned.

"Fox hunting?"

Tindal smirked. "Well, it's trail hunting, you're aware of that?"

"Hmm." Yvonne tapped her pen on her chin. "When did you last see Krysta, Trevor?"

"Ooh, wait a minute... A while ago, maybe six months, give or take a few weeks."

"What was she doing when you saw her?"

"She was with some friends, trying to disrupt a trail hunt, and she had a set-to with the boss."

"With Tunicliffe?"

"Yes. Got heated, too. He tried to mow some of them down with his Land Rover."

"Did they report him?"

"I don't know. I expect they did. They are always reporting him for something."

"Were you aware Krysta was in danger? Did you ever suspect Mr Tunicliffe of hurting a protester or of being capable of that?"

"No. He's all bluster. He has his moments, but never witnessed him hurting anyone."

"What about you?"

"Me?"

"Have you ever hurt anyone?"

"No. I try to keep myself to myself and do my job and get my wages at the end of the month. I like what I do and I don't look to pick fights with anyone."

"Where were you on the morning Krysta Whyte was killed?"

"At home in the cottage, or checking on the pheasants and fencing around the pens. There is always repair work to do. It's a large estate."

"A trail hunt took place that day. Did you have a role in it?"

"No. The kennels take care of the dogs and Mr Tunicliffe likes to organise and run everything, himself. He has security guys, who I think are just local lads he bungs a few bob too. There's no call for me to get involved."

"And you didn't observe Krysta around on that day?"

Tindall shook his head. "No, I didn't."

The Kettle shrilled in their ears and Yvonne rose from her seat. "We may need to speak to you again, Trevor. How do we contact you? Do you have a phone number?"

He shook his head. "No signal on my mobile here, but you can ring the main house if you need me. Someone would get a message to me."

"I appreciate that. Well, It's been good talking with you and sorry, again, for losing your niece. I want to assure you we are doing everything we can to find her killer."

He nodded. "Thank you. That's good to know."

"One more thing." Yvonne spoke to him from the doorway. "Do you have access to a vehicle?"

He nodded. I have a pickup. "It's ten years old, but goes a treat. It's round the back."

"May we see it?" She asked, noticing that Dewi was already heading over to it.

"Sure. I'll show you."

A dark green pickup stood in the small yard at the back of the property. It looked good for its age, well-kept.

She peered over the sides. In the back lay a spare tyre, a shovel and two jerry cans. No blankets.

She joined Dewi, as he looked inside the cab which was bare, save for a pair of sunglasses left on the dash.

"Our forensic team may give this the once over." She addressed Tindall.

"Oh?" he asked, his eyes narrowed.

"We believe someone transported Krysta in a vehicle and we are examining vehicles in and around the area."

Tindall nodded. "You have a job to do. I'm all right with that. Anything that helps."

8

AN UNEXPECTED ILLNESS

Early buds sprouted forth and the hedgerows and trees had taken on a vibrant green, heralding that precious time when spring becomes summer. It was a day to feel energised and happy.

Yvonne filled her lungs with the scents of the season. They were making headway with the Krysta Whyte case, leads increasing by the day, and her physical health had improved so much she no longer needed a walking aid of any kind and could get around without major twinges.

She sang along with the car radio, as she swung into the front yard of Tasha's cottage and parked up. They had discussed a weekend visit a few weeks prior, but Yvonne had set off that morning without informing her friend. Not that she hadn't tried to let her know. Tasha's phone was off and the cottage lacked a landline. If the psychologist wasn't home, the DI would head to town. There, she could have a spot of lunch and a walk along the beach. Either way, it was a win-win on such a sublime day.

Yvonne knocked on the cottage door and waited. When there was no answer, she tried the handle and found it to be unlocked. Good. The psychologist was somewhere around.

"Hello? Tasha?" She set her handbag down on the coffee table in the orderly lounge and walked to the sliding glass doors that led to the beach. They were open two inches.

"Tasha?" She pushed them wide enough to walk through, before closing them behind her. Most likely, her friend had gone for a walk.

She would head down the beach to the ocean. If she didn't bump into Tasha, and the psychologist returned to the cottage, she would find Yvonne's bag and realise the DI was around. Whatever happened, Yvonne suspected they would find each other at some point. It was Saturday. They had all the time they needed. Taking off her shoes, she left them beside the glass doors, liking the coolness of the sand beneath her feet as she wandered over the grass-spiked dunes.

She could smell fish and hear the hiss of the ocean long before she topped the sandy humps to see it. The DI filled her lungs with the scent and her ears with the sound, as she stood atop the dunes, lifting herself up on tiptoes, and stretching her arms skyward.

It was then, she saw a hunched figure where the sea met the shore, kneeling and bent over, and dressed in white. She headed that way.

As she neared, the figure sat upright, staring out to sea.
"Tasha?"
The chocolate head turned to her. "Yvonne?"
The DI ran towards where her friend was kneeling in the sand. "Are you okay? What are you doing?"
The psychologist wiped a sleeve across her face before turning towards Yvonne. "I'm fine." She smiled, but her eyes were unfocussed and red-rimmed. She looked lost.

"You are so obviously *not* fine." Yvonne knelt beside her friend. "What is it, Tasha? I have never seen you this distressed. Please, tell me what's wrong?" She placed an arm around the psychologist's shoulders.

Tasha sighed, her body shuddering. "It's my dad, Yvonne. Consultants have told him that he has advanced pancreatic cancer. They said it's inoperable."

"Oh no! Oh my God, Tasha, I am so sorry. That is awful news." Yvonne twisted Tasha around to give her a full hug.

Tasha's voice choked. "I'm leaving tomorrow, for Kent. The first train I can get. I'll be staying at my mum's house in Ashford for two or three weeks. She said they are waiting for a hospice place to become available for my dad. He's in a hospital in Canterbury at the moment."

"Oh, Tasha..."

The psychologist lifted her face to the DI's. "Why has he so little time left? How is that even fair?"

"I will drive you to Kent..." Yvonne offered, and meant it, as she wiped a stray tear from her friend's cheek.

Tasha shook her head. "I know you would do that for me and I thank you for it, but it's not practical, Yvonne. You have a job to do. I will be in Kent until... until..."

"Hey, hey, shush." Yvonne held her friend tight as Tasha let out a sob. "Whatever you need, okay? If you need something or you want anything sorted at your cottage, tell me what and I will do it. It is no trouble."

Tasha nodded. "Thank you."

"In the meantime, I will stay tonight. I packed a bag. It's in the car. I had thought we might get drunk."

The psychologist gave her a weak smile. "We still might..."

9

PREY

In his mind, his wings arched high above him. Skin and feather melted into one, tented purity and brilliance, dazzling all below. Then, spreading wide, casting an ominous shadow on all before as he homed in on the creatures of the woods. Creatures who believed they were protecting a world in which they could protect nothing. This was his space. Before him, space invaders. Prey.

He checked his watch. Eight-thirty-seven. Mini binoculars back to his eyes, he counted twelve people on the ground. All eco veterans. First to the fray and always the most vocal at any protest.

The tallest of them, six-foot-two, give or take an inch, looked an obvious ringleader, striding about handing out placards and strategically placing bodies around the gates to the site.

Uncombed and unwashed. Definitely a die-hard. Approximate age, thirty. He wouldn't be an easy takedown, but that was all part of the challenge. He'd take longer to die. There was a satisfaction in that.

He took a bite of his homemade chicken sandwich, eyes

watering as the hot pepper sauce bit into his tongue. It kept him focussed.

Having chosen his next victim, all he had to do was look him up on the net, make contact, and set up a fake cause with the need for a meeting. A meeting, he'd make sure, his intended victim would not want to miss.

10

WHAT FRIENDS ARE FOR

Yvonne grabbed her overnight bag and a wine carrier, containing two bottles of chardonnay and a bottle of tequila, placing them on the ground while she slammed the car boot shut.

Car keys in her mouth, she carried them through the door and into the kitchen.

"I'll take your bag through to the bedroom," Tasha said as she picked it up to carry it through.

"I will cook you a decent meal." Yvonne called after her. "And pour you a large glass of chardonnay, which you will not refuse."

Tasha returned, eyes puffy, but grinning despite herself. "What would I do without you? You improve my mood, even in circumstances like these."

"You'd better believe it." Yvonne answered, clattering pans from cupboard to stove.

"I hope I don't offend you if I can't manage much," Tasha said, eyeing the largest of the pans.

The DI popped a cork and poured a generous helping of

chardonnay into two glasses, one of which she handed to Tasha. "Here, you go. This will give you an appetite and help lift your spirits. You can't do anything until tomorrow, and the wine might help stop you going stir-crazy."

"And give me a lovely hangover for the train." Tasha grimaced.

"I can make you an anti-hangover breakfast. You'll be fine." Yvonne winked.

"Oh, boy." Tasha rolled her eyes in mock indignation, before her face and voice took on a gravity that stopped the DI in her tracks. "I'm glad you came. When I saw you called, I intended returning your call once I'd gotten myself together. I'm glad you chose today to surprise me."

∽

THEIR MEAL COMPRISED pasta with bacon, in a garlic cream and white wine sauce. Tasha ate what she could, which wasn't much. She eyed the rest on her plate before lifting her eyes to Yvonne's, an apologetic look within them.

The DI smiled and patted her friend's hand. "Don't worry. I'm glad you've eaten something, at least."

Tasha put down her knife and fork. "I wish I could have done it justice. That was truly delicious." She gave a wistful smile. "If you were not such a brilliant detective, I could imagine you as a chef."

"Oh, go on with you." Yvonne pulled a face.

"Seriously. I'd employ you."

Yvonne giggled. "More wine?"

Tasha stared at her near-empty glass. "I guess one more won't hurt."

Yvonne refilled their glasses.

Angel of Death

"My dad hasn't had it easy in life." Tasha ran her fingers around the rim of her glass.

Yvonne seated herself, head tilted.

"He and my mum have had their share of trials. They split up a few times, in the distant past." The psychologist looked her friend in the eye. "He always took it hardest. My mum has a fiery temper. All vocal and flailing arms. She has Italian blood in her."

"Did she hit your dad?"

"Oh no." Tasha shook her head. "Nothing like that. But she'd walk out, or else send him packing. Each time, she would be adamant she meant it. Then, a month or several later, she'd be back, or she'd phone him up to ask him to come home."

"Wow." Yvonne tilted her head, searching Tasha's face. "That must have been hard for you, especially when you were young."

Tasha sighed. "Gave me more than a few sleepless nights, until I was older and got used to it."

"Were you angry with her?"

"Not when I was young. When she walked out, I missed her terribly. But, as a teenager, I resented her for it. I resented her for the way it affected our feelings. Mine and dad's. I thought her childish. It was as though I was older than her. More mature. Then, one day, she stopped doing it. Just stopped either running out on us, or sending my dad packing. It was like she had suddenly grown up. Realised the hurt she'd caused. The last time they split, I was sixteen and revising for exams."

"Were your results affected?"

"Maybe, a little. I remember dad talking to her when she came back. I overheard part of the conversation. He asked her if she had even considered the effect her behaviour was having on me and my future and, from her responses, I don't think she had. Whatever he said to her, it worked. She never went that far again. Not to my knowledge, anyway. They've been together nearly forty years and, for the last twenty-or-so, they haven't split up once."

"How did she take the news of...?" Yvonne's voice trailed away as though she was reticent of reminding Tasha.

"Of my dad's illness? She was in bits on the phone. It hit her hard. I'm sorry for her. She loves him. She loves him very much. I don't doubt it."

The DI nodded. "She'll value your presence and support."

Tasha nodded. "I know."

They spent the rest of the evening talking, drinking and, on occasions, crying until, both exhausted, they fell asleep.

∽

"What can I get you? Hello?"

Yvonne jumped as she realized the young male behind the counter awaited her attention, the people in front of her having gotten their beverages and dissipated.

She closed the gap between herself and the male. "Oh, I'm sorry." She cast her eyes over the chalked list on the blackboard behind and above him. "Two large lattes, please." She pulled her purse from her bag, listening as a female voice came over the tannoy, announcing that the train to Birmingham New Street would arrive in ten minutes, stopping at Machynlleth and Shrewsbury.

The fishy-tang of the sea wafted through Aberdovey station as Yvonne thought of the six-hour journey that Tasha would have to make, changing at Birmingham, and again at Reading and Staines before reaching Ashford. A journey far too long when one was feeling as distressed as her friend was.

The sound of air whooshing through hot milk pierced her thoughts and she realised she was still standing in front of the counter, waiting for the coffees and searching for words to comfort the psychologist.

"That'll be six pounds seventy." The young man placed lids onto the coffee cups and pushed them towards her.

"Thank you." She placed the right money on the counter, giving the barista a smile before pushing her bag strap back onto her shoulder and grabbing the cups.

Outside, Tasha sat on a pale-blue bench, shoulders hunched, her glazed eyes staring out over the tracks.

At a quarter past one, the station had filled with people waiting to catch the thirteen-twenty-two train.

As the DI approached, the psychologist appeared not to notice anyone around her, continuing to stare, a haunted expression in her sunken eyes.

Yvonne placed the coffee cups down next to her friend, seating herself the opposite side of her.

She still hadn't found the right words and decided they were unnecessary. Instead, she placed an arm around Tasha's shoulders, pulling her close.

Tasha's head fell to rest on her shoulder.

From the corner of her eye, the DI saw a tear drip into her lap, just before the tannoy announced the thirteen-twenty-two as it screeched into the station.

"Are you going to be all right?" Yvonne had the urge to climb on board with her.

The psychologist looked up and accepted the coffee the DI held out. "Yes. Yes, I'll be all right." She ran a sleeve under her nose.

"Call me, when you get there?"

Tasha nodded, running the back of her hand across her eyes. "Thank you."

Yvonne closed both eyelids in acknowledgement as her friend turned and boarded the train.

11

KRYSTA

Yvonne and Dewi paused on the threshold of a substantial detached home near Mochdre, two miles to the West of Newtown. The DI guessed it must be four or five bedrooms, at least.

Although an enclosed property, someone had left the tall metal gates unlocked, anticipating their arrival. Dewi exited the car to push them open, allowing Yvonne to park on the ample driveway. To the right hand-side of the red-brick property, she spied the steps of a swimming pool, the bulk of which disappeared behind the house. The well-kept lawns matched the paved driveway, in their perfect condition. The sun seemed to bounce around the whole, giving the place a Mediterranean feel.

Dewi pressed the intercom and announced their arrival. A sharp buzz, and the brilliant-white door opened with a click.

A middle-aged man, dressed in casual trousers and shirt, came to greet them. He was well built and the DI eyed his muscles; the gravitas in his blue eyes hinted at intelligence and a profound sadness.

She held her hand out for him to shake. "DI Yvonne Giles." She pointed to her DS. "And this is Sergeant Dewi Hughes."

"Miles. Miles Whyte. Krysta's father." He accepted her hand. "Thank you for coming. My wife Kate is in the garden out back." He turned to lead them through a huge open-plan kitchen-diner.

Yvonne cast her eyes around. Their home could be the centre spread in some style magazine, all shiny surfaces and doors without handles. Light bouncing around the interior and giving the space an air of being outside, helped by the massive glass doors to the garden which, like walls, stood open with a decked patio area between. The latter had a good-sized swimming pool sunk into it.

Miles led them into the quarter-of-an-acre garden, surrounded by evergreen hedges and dotted with mature trees and clever planting.

Kate Whyte appeared fragile, tendrils of greying-blonde hair falling about her face from a loosely held ponytail. Hands inside the pockets of her pale-blue summer dress, she rose to greet them. Perhaps emphasised by her lack of makeup, her skin appeared pale and colourless, her expression, haunted.

"You have a beautiful home." Yvonne smiled at her.

"Thank you." Kate smiled back, but there was no joy in it.

Yvonne took her hand. "I'm so sorry about your daughter."

Kate nodded, turning her gaze towards the trees at the end of the garden, tears forming in her amber eyes. "We still have the swings we bought her for her Seventh birthday."

Yvonne cast her gaze towards the frame at the end of the garden, under the trees, spying the telltale signs of age; the red plastic seats now more pink and white. Patches of rust dotting the black metal frame.

"We will find out who killed her." Yvonne's voice was firm, her gaze determined. "We have to ask you some questions."

Miles walked over to his wife, putting an arm around her waist before they seated themselves. Yvonne and Dewi sat opposite, across a glass outdoor table.

"What would you like to know?" Miles held his wife's hand.

"How much did you see of Krysta in the weeks preceding her death?" Yvonne's tone was soft.

Miles ran a hand through his hair. "Not at all, in the week before she died. She came here for Sunday lunch the weekend before that."

"Was her boyfriend with her?"

"Ed?" Miles shook his head. "No. He didn't always come with her and, for whatever reason, that day he didn't."

"How did she seem while she was here?"

"Quiet." Kate spoke up, leaning her elbow on the arm of her chair and cradling her chin. "Lost in her own thoughts."

"Did you get any indication of what she was thinking about?"

Kate shook her head.

"You didn't ask her?"

Kate sighed, a wistful, pained expression in her eyes. "No. I wish we had. You've no idea..." Her voice tailed off.

"What about before that? When had you seen her prior to that day?"

"She came round the Saturday before. Not for lunch, that time. She stayed long enough to collect something from her room."

"From her room? I assumed she was living with Ed?" Yvonne frowned.

"She was. But we kept her room open for her, in case she needed it. Her room from childhood... She was fluid in her living arrangements. She came back to stay here many times, since leaving home. Usually, after a break-up or some other traumatic or troubling period in her life." Miles flicked a glance towards his wife.

"How was she on that Saturday?"

"She seemed fine. In reasonable spirits and talking about the proposed wind farms near Abermule. She was happy that they had denied the planning permission, at least for the time being. Yeah, it buoyed her up for a while."

"She got involved in the campaign against the wind farms?"

Miles nodded. "She pretty-much headed it up. Helped to draw up the campaign plans, and she didn't miss a single gathering."

"I see. Did she express fear over the campaign? Especially, regarding those she was campaigning against?"

Miles pursed his lips. "Not that I recall. I mean, she had had run-ins with representatives at the meetings, but she didn't express a fear about the meetings or the people involved."

"Would she have told you? I mean, if she had?"

He tilted his head. "I'm not sure, Inspector."

"Did she talk to you about Ed, at all? About their relationship, or her intentions?"

"Krysta talked to me about him." Kate frowned as she remembered. "She thought he'd been distant, distracted by something. She tried talking to him about it, but he would close the conversation down and she was afraid they were drifting apart and there appeared to be little she could do to change that."

"What did she come to collect? Any ideas?"

"Her diary."

"Her diary?"

"Yes."

"We didn't find a diary. Where did she keep it?"

"Here." Kate tilted her head, her eyes locked on the DI. "She felt it was safe from prying eyes, here in her room."

"You don't think she would have kept it at the place she was sharing with Ed?"

Kate shook her head. "She wrote everything in it. From what she was doing, to her inner thoughts and fears about her relationship. She wouldn't have wanted Ed to witness that private part of her. I wondered if her worries were born out of a general anxiety. Whatever, she wanted no one reading them."

"What about you?" Yvonne asked Kate. "Did you see inside her diary."

"No, Inspector. I would never have invaded her privacy like that. Even, when she was little. I wouldn't have looked without asking."

"So, you don't know if she had written about any specific worries in her last few weeks?"

"No, I'm sorry."

"That's okay. Now we know it exists, we'll look for her diary and will return it to you, when we have finished with it."

"Thank you." Kate smiled, tears in her eyes.

"Could we see her room, please?"

Miles stood. "Of course, I'll take you to it."

Yvonne and Dewi got up to follow him, the DI looking

round towards Kate. "Thank you for talking to us. I will keep you informed. We'll do our best to find out who killed her and we will bring them to justice."

Kate nodded. "Thank you, DI Giles."

∼

Krysta's room was off-white and yet another light-filled, spacious room with sliding doors leading onto a small balcony overlooking the garden and swimming pool.

Various items of Krysta's lay in a muddle on the bed, on the sideboard and bedside cabinet, including books, pens and pencils, notes and plans, and a laptop.

A khaki coat lay over the back of an office chair.

Yvonne took out her mobile and photographed everything. "Our SOCO officers will need to take some of these items, including the laptop."

"Yes. They can help themselves." Miles nodded. "Anything to help find her killer."

"Thank you." Yvonne reached into her bag. "Here is my number. If you remember anything else you think important, I want you to call me. Any time, night or day."

Miles accepted the card before glancing around the room. "We miss her so much. Everything is... empty. I wish I'd talked to her more. You forget to make the most of those you love, take for granted the years that seem to stretch out ahead, assuming that they will keep coming through the door. And then, one day, they don't."

Yvonne saw the broken expression on his face and the weight in his hunched shoulders and had the urge to comfort him. She rubbed his arm. "From what you've told me, Krysta viewed this as her sanctuary. She knew you loved and supported her." The DI shouldered her bag. "Help your wife. She needs you and you need her."

He nodded.

"Thank you for your time, Mr Whyte. We'll let ourselves out."

12

EVA WILDE

As she knocked on the paint-chipped door of Ed and Krysta's eclectic cottage, it reminded Yvonne of the stark contrast in living conditions of the dead girl and her parents. The DI mused over whether Krysta would have felt more comfortable in the relaxed mess of the cottage, even if needing the support of her mother and father. From what she had learned, Yvonne suspected this was the case.

Ed came to the door in jeans and a loose grey t-shirt, the front of which bore telltale holes from cigarette ash.

"Can we come in?" Yvonne asked, as Ed filled the door frame.

He stared at them, as though unsure.

"It won't take long." Dewi took a step forward, to stand beside the DI.

Ed took a step back, sighing and running a hand through lank hair. "Sure." A redness spread along his neck, into his face.

Behind him, a young woman of about twenty, with long

Angel of Death

red hair and wearing a flowery cotton dress, grabbed her coat and bag.

"Hello." Dewi blocked the doorway. "I'm DS Dewi Hughes. Can I ask your name, miss?"

The young woman cast a nervous glance towards Ed.

He said nothing, rubbing his face and neck.

"E-Eva." The girl stuttered. "Eva Wilde."

"Are you able to talk to us?" Dewi stepped away from the door.

"I'm sorry." She looked at him, wide-eyed. "I've got an appointment. It's urgent."

The Sergeant nodded and allowed her past. "We will need to speak to you at some point, soon though, Eva."

She nodded. "Ed has my number." With that, she left.

Yvonne turned her attention back to Ed, who looked at his shoes, shuffling between his feet, his face still red.

"Are you two seeing each other?" She asked, keeping her tone light.

"We're friends." He ran his tongue across his lips. "She's been helping me sort everything, since Krysta..."

"I see. It's just, you looked-"

"We like each other. That's all."

"Were you two friends while Krysta was alive?"

Ed nodded. "We talked to each other, but not that much."

Yvonne rubbed her chin. "Ed, we wanted to ask you if you knew that Krysta had a diary?" She studied his face.

"No." He stared at her, his eyes wide. "What diary?"

"Her parents said she kept a diary and a relative informed us that she had it with her, either here, or on her person, at the time someone murdered her."

"Wow. I wasn't aware." He turned to glance around the room, as though the mess of books and papers, cups and clothes, would yield up the mysterious artefact.

"So, you didn't see one?"

Ed frowned. "Honestly, I didn't even know she had one. Your officers searched this place. If she had one here, they would have found it." He shrugged.

"Might anyone else have taken it from here? Eva, perhaps?"

"Eva? No. What would Eva want with my dead girlfriend's diary?"

"What about anyone else?"

"Well, I have had friends in here, the usual crew, but I can't see any of them running off with Krysta's diary."

"Can you give us the names of all the people who have visited you, since Krysta's death?"

"Sure, but you already have the names. It's our sab group. No one else comes here."

Yvonne nodded. "May we take a seat?"

"Er, yeah." Ed ran his hands through his hair. "Sorry, your visit took me by surprise. Please, do take a seat." He moved over to the couch, joined by the officers.

Yvonne looked at the filled ashtray, fighting an urge to take it and empty it. The smell of it was making her ill. "Ed, someone told us that you've been having a relationship with Eva for some time and that the affair began while Krysta was still alive."

Ed looked at the floor, colour once again rising in his neck.

"Did it?"

"No, I... Yes. Yes, it did."

"How long ago?"

"Oh, well, I... four months, maybe?"

"Four months before Krysta's death?"

"About that."

"Was Krysta aware?"

"No. Not to my knowledge, anyway."

"Could she have suspected?"

He shrugged, looking away. "She said nothing about it to me."

"Did her behaviour towards you change?"

"Well, I told you we were cooling off with a view to breaking up. It's just... Well, it is sometimes... hard. It's difficult to cut ties with someone."

"Why didn't you tell her about Eva?"

"I didn't want to hurt her. I don't suppose you'll believe me, but I felt bad, going behind her back, and I didn't want to argue with her, either. She could be..."

"What?"

"Unstable."

"Unstable? In what way?"

"Well, she could blow up on occasions. Out of the blue. I was a coward, and I didn't want to be on the receiving end of her anger."

"What did Eva think about that?"

"Eva? She would have preferred it if I had told Krysta, that was clear."

"Are you serious about Eva?"

"Yeah." He shrugged.

"You don't sound too sure."

"It's only been a few months. I mean, if it had continued for a few more months while Krysta was alive, I would have spoken to Krysta about it and packed my bags."

"Where did Krysta keep her things, Ed?"

"Most of her stuff is in our bedroom upstairs."

"May we go up there?"

"Well, you can, but like I said, your officers already went through her belongings."

"Are some of her things still here?"

"Yes, they are. Although they won't be for much longer. I can't hang on to them forever. I thought I would return some things to her parents."

Ed led them up the narrow stairway to a small bedroom at the top. The unmade double bed took up half of the space which seemed smaller than it was, because of a large wardrobe which dominated the room. On the floor lay piles of clothing, some of which looked like they belonged to a female.

"Are those Krysta's?" Yvonne cast her eyes over them.

Ed rubbed his forehead. "No. They're Eva's." He didn't meet her eyes.

"Where are Krysta's things?"

Ed nodded towards a leather armchair in the corner, on which various items such as books and clothing lay mingled together.

"Do you mind if we look?"

Ed shrugged. "Help yourself."

"Could you give us a moment?"

"Sure." Ed paused, his mouth open to say more. He closed it again.

After he left the room, Yvonne flicked through Krysta's books, in case someone had missed the diary.

Dewi opened the wardrobe doors to look inside.

"Anything?" Yvonne asked him.

He rattled the hangers. "Nothing in here except Ed's clothes, by the looks. What about you?"

"Nothing." Yvonne sat on the edge of the bed, her brow furrowed, two brochures in her hands. "Found these, though."

Dewi walked over to her. "What are they?"

"Well, this looks like the plans for a leisure complex on the outskirts of town. It's talking about taking advantage of

Angel of Death

the improved access due to the new bypass." She handed him the top brochure. "Bannerman Holdings."

"Wow. I didn't even know the company existed."

"Hmm. And this one, is from Futurecon Energy, the firm that wants to set up new wind farms in the area."

"Well, how about that? Looks as though she had a few environmental protests pending before she died."

"But were they motives for her death? I'll speak to Ed. I think we'll hang onto these."

~

Eva's long red hair reflected her surname, like she had been out in a gale for an hour. Yvonne suspected, she used her chaotic hair to hide her eyes when she wished to avoid scrutiny or, perhaps, felt shy.

Trying to gauge the woman's thoughts was like waiting for badgers to come out of their set. Just when she thought she might get a glimpse, they disappeared back inside.

Eva's cheeks and chin sported copious freckles, as did her forearms. Her nails were bitten to the quick and her legs wrapped around each other, crossing at both the thigh and the ankles.

They sat on a bench in the park, near to where Eva had been helping man a stall, aimed at recruiting more people to the saboteur cause. Eva had left it in the care of a friend whilst she and the DI talked.

Yvonne cleared her throat. "Thank you for speaking to us, Eva. You know why we're here?"

Eva clicked the knuckles of her left hand. "You're looking into the death of Ed's ex-girlfriend."

"Krysta. Yes, that's right. What have you heard about that?"

Eva pulled at her lips, taking a few moments to consider. "Only that they found her in the woods, nailed to a tree." She shrugged.

"Did you know her, Eva?" Yvonne tilted her head.

"Kind of."

"Kind of?"

"Well, I met her a few times, but I never talked to her. I'd fallen for Ed and was uncomfortable seeing Krysta as it seemed two-faced to talk to her. I didn't want to be her friend, knowing I would betray her friendship."

Yvonne caught Eva's eye. "That is decent of you. What did you make of Ed two-timing Krysta? Did you suppose he might do the same to you one day?"

Eva shrugged.

"Did you worry your affair wouldn't last?"

Eva chewed the inside of her cheek.

"Eva?"

"I didn't worry. I like him and I wasn't considering the longer term."

"Did Krysta suspect Ed of seeing you? Did she voice suspicions?"

"No. At least, I wasn't aware, if she did. She seemed comfortable around him. She didn't notice me. Not in that way. I doubt it crossed her mind that Ed would want to date someone like me."

"Why?"

"She was beautiful."

"You shouldn't put yourself down." Yvonne sighed. "What about Ed? Did Ed speak to you about Krysta?"

Eva nodded.

"What did he say? Did he mention leaving her?"

"He said he would. Told me he was getting up the courage to do it."

Angel of Death

"When did he tell you that?"

"Oh, I can't remember, maybe a few weeks before Krysta died."

"And he never confirmed saying anything to her?"

Eva shook her head. "No. No, he did not."

"Where were you, on the morning that Krysta disappeared?"

Eva uncrossed her legs, crossing them again on the opposite side. "I was with the Shropshires. I mean, the Shropshire hunt saboteurs, planning where each of us would be during the hunt."

"What time did Ed join you?"

"Hmm, As far as I can remember, it was around eleven in the morning. He was late because he waited for Krysta, who didn't arrive." Eva blushed, her head bowed. "For obvious reasons." The last, was almost a whisper.

"Could Ed have been involved in Krysta's death, in your opinion?"

"What? No. No. He wouldn't do anything like that. Never." She looked up, allowing Yvonne to see both her eyes, which were wide and determined.

"You seem very sure."

"Look, Ed's heart wasn't in the relationship anymore, but he would not have wanted to harm Krysta. None of us would. Don't you get it? We care about the lives of creatures and people. We love all living things. We're not about taking life, but about saving it. We care, you get it?"

At that moment, Yvonne fancied she could see into the girl's soul. She sensed that Eva believed everything she said and nodded. "Can you come into the station to give a formal statement about that day's events and all the things you've just told me?"

Eva nodded. "Yes, of course I can. When do you want me to come?"

"This afternoon?"

Eva nodded. "I can be there about three-thirty, once we've finished here."

Yvonne rose to leave. "Thank you, Eva."

13

DEATH STRIKES TWICE

The wind pushed and pulled at their car as a flurry of hailstones fell from a sky filled with every variety of cloud.

Yvonne's nails left painful indentations in her palms, so intense was the way she balled her fists. Fifteen minutes earlier, a call had come through to say they had found another body. This time it was a male in the woods above Castell-Y-Dail, a small holding near Newtown.

The DI's worst fear realised. No longer was this a simple case of finding out who Krysta's potential enemies were. The DI recognised the signs, she'd been here before. Pray God she was wrong, and this wasn't another serial case.

They were one of the first cars to arrive and, much to Yvonne's chagrin, had to hang back until SOCO had secured the site and set out the designated walkways. The ambulance and medics left the scene, having confirmed death.

After kicking their heels for half-an-hour, Yvonne and Dewi suited up, when allowed to enter the inner cordon where the body leaned against the base of a pine tree.

Pathologist Roger Hanson knelt by the victim, talking to another member of his team.

Yvonne walked over. "They killed him in the same way they killed Krysta Whyte?" She crouched alongside.

Hanson nodded. "Back and arms broken. Hands nailed together to the tree and this..." Hanson pointed to the feather between the victim's legs.

"Sorry, excuse me, could I-" The photographer looked at her, grimacing. "Sorry," he repeated.

"No problem." The DI's knees clicked as she stood and moved to the side.

The male victim had sustained extensive bruising to the left side of his head.

"Did he put up a fight?" Yvonne asked Hanson.

"It looks like he could have done. In which case, the killer may also have sustained injuries. Something to consider when you're examining suspects."

The victim's eyes lay open. He was facing the ground, his head having fallen forward at the time of death. His clothing dishevelled, he had lost the top two buttons of his shirt, which hung open. His short, curly hair appeared sweat-soaked and, as with Krysta, the flesh of the hands had torn around the nail as he tried to free himself.

"Same MO. Same signature." Yvonne sighed. "Damn."

"I don't envy you." Hanson was busy transferring swabs and samples into vials.

The DI shifted her gaze to the countryside around. "If this victim fought with his killer, we might get DNA. We got nothing from Krysta. Any evidence of skin under his nails?"

Hanson shook his head. "Nothing obvious, but I've swabbed them and will swab them again in the lab, once we get the body back. Do you have an identity?"

"No." Yvonne stood. "I expect we'll know by the end of the day, though. I'll let you know."

∼

Callum and Dai greeted her when she got back to the station.

Dai pushed his pen behind his ear. Sleeves rolled up, he read from the notes in his iPad. "The body found this morning was that of Terry Lloyd, aged twenty-nine and from the Barnfields area of Newtown, where he'd been living with his mum, Michelle. His dad is deceased."

"Living with his mum? Not in a relationship, then?"

Dai shook his head. "He was in a relationship until about eight months ago when he and his girlfriend split up. Mrs Lloyd, his mum, said the split was amicable, and they remained on friendly terms."

"Children?"

"No. They had a miscarriage a few months prior to the split. I checked out the ex-partner, and she isn't and wasn't in the area at the time the killer murdered Terry. She's living and working in Cardiff and never involved herself in his environmental protests."

"Wait, he was an environmentalist, too?" Yvonne cocked her head, brow furrowed.

"Yeah, sorry, I should have said."

"No, that's all right. So, we found a tentative link with the first victim, they both protested countryside issues. Can we confirm whether they knew each other?"

"We've been looking at whether they did, ma'am and it's not looking like it at the moment, but there are a few more calls to make, so I'll keep you posted."

"Ok, good. Also, find out if Terry had any run-ins with

anyone. Anyone whose back he might have gotten up. We've got two murders with the same MO and signature. The killer may have been an opportunist serial killer but, with two environmental protesters killed, it would appear there's more to it. If you find anything significant, I want it, okay?"

"Fair enough."

Callum caught her arm just as she was about to go. "Sorry, I almost forgot, they found fibres on Krysta's clothing which do not belong to her. Two red fibres. They've checked Ed's place and there is nothing red in the furnishings. They've taken a red jumper belonging to Ed for examination as the fibres are from a woollen item, most likely a jumper or blanket. The jumper was at the back of Ed's wardrobe and he claims not to have worn it for eighteen months to two years. Said he had forgotten it was there as he shrunk it in the wash a long time ago. So, he said."

"Okay, well, keep following that up. I suppose it's possible she may have taken an item from Ed's wardrobe that had been in contact with the jumper?"

"Not, according to Ed, ma'am. He reckons Krysta never went into his wardrobe. She kept her things separate from his. SOCO took all the clothing from both Ed and her parents' homes for comparison."

"Okay, good work, Callum."

"Thank you, ma'am."

~

Yvonne made herself a coffee at the tiny table housing the kettle at the back of CID, stirring for longer than warranted while she mulled over the day's events. She could still see Terry Lloyd propped up against the tree, head lolled forward, the telltale evidence of his final struggle etched on his face. He joined Krysta in the DI's waking thoughts and nightmares. The sinking feeling in the pit of her stomach was a familiar one. She would need to dig deep, again."

The tremor in her right hand as she stirred her coffee reminded her that she needed to eat something.

As if reading her thoughts, Dewi came up behind her. "I'm just nipping out to get a sandwich. Do you want anything?"

She pursed her lips. "I ought to. I don't know how much I'll manage, but I should try to eat. Could I trouble you to get a cheese and onion roll for me? I'll make you a cuppa for when you get back."

Her sergeant nodded. "Tea would be great, thanks."

As Dewi left to get food, she sipped her drink and thought of Tasha. Up until now, she'd had little time to worry about her friend. Desperate to find out how she was, Yvonne took her mobile phone out of her bag and stared at it. Dare she ring? Would it be a good time? She flipped through her contacts and tapped on Tasha's name, hitting the green button as the number appeared. But, before anyone could answer, she tapped on the red button and stopped the call. Something in her gut told her it was a bad time. She put the phone back in her bag.

14

THE FAVOUR

It was much later that evening, when she found the courage to ring her friend, standing outside her house, where the signal was a little better. It was still blowing a gale, but at least it was dry, if somewhat cold.

"How is he?" Yvonne turned away from the wind, mobile phone pressed tight to her ear.

"He's so damned stoic about it all." Tasha sighed. "I'm amazed at how serene he is, actually. I can't imagine being that brave if I were in his shoes."

"Incredible... And your mum?"

"Hasn't stopped crying. She hopes for a miracle; asking the doctors for second opinions, clutching at straws and I don't blame her."

"What about you?" Yvonne's voice was almost a whisper.

"Don't worry about me." Tasha sighed down the phone. "I'm sure you've got enough on your plate."

"That's not the same thing." Yvonne wanted to say something more, but the right words failed her as everything she thought of sounded inadequate. Glib, even.

"They're moving dad tomorrow. He's going into a hospice

near Canterbury. He'll be much more comfortable in a hospice. It's busy where he is at the moment. The chaos confuses him, so many people coming and going."

After a two-second pause, Yvonne looked at her shoes, asking, "Is there anything I can do? I thought I might drop by the cottage. Check everything is all right. Can I do anything specific for you at the cottage?"

"If you can afford the time. There may be some post in the letter box and I can't remember whether I locked the sliding doors."

"It's no problem and will be a pleasure. I feel so helpless here, it will be a relief to do something practical for you."

"If you need it, a spare key is hidden in the middle pot of the potting tray, in the greenhouse out the back. If you are driving to Aberdovey, the least I can do is make sure you have a cup of tea and a bite to eat. Just help yourself to whatever."

"Thank you."

"I'd better go."

Yvonne cleared her throat. "Get some rest when you can. Look after yourself."

"I will."

Yvonne ended the call, looking across the fields to the hills behind. "I miss you," she whispered.

∽

YVONNE PULLED on the sliding doors, but Tasha had remembered to lock them before leaving for Ashford. She headed round the back, to the tiny greenhouse where the psychologist had planted various seedlings in a large tray. The antique metal-and-glass door rattled on its hinges as she pushed it open.

A tiny island in the centre held a large potting tray. As promised, the centre pot yielded up a Yale key with tiny clumps of compost still clinging to it.

Yvonne wiped it with a finger, before taking it back to the front of the house and opening the door from the yard.

The cottage felt odd. Unfamiliar. All silent and cold. The chill wind blowing off the sea had sapped any heat imbued by the sun's rays through the tiny gaps in the ageing windows and under the doors.

She thought about putting the heating on, but decided against it, instead, heating leftover milk in the microwave to make hot chocolate and allowing its thick warmth to rejuvenate her.

The post, she left next to the kettle ready for Tasha's return, there having been nothing amongst it which screamed urgent to her.

On the mantle were family photographs including one of Tasha as a child of around five years old. In it, she wore a cute pair of dungarees covered in mud, the same mud which caked the tiny hands she held up for the camera; a cheeky smile lighting her face. Yvonne lifted the photo frame, running her fingertips over the smiling girl before replacing it, her attention taken by a photo of Tasha's parents. Arms around one another, they leaned against a fence somewhere in the countryside. The DI remembered meeting Mr and Mrs Phillips, the time the Priest Killer abducted Tasha. How terrified they were and how relieved when they got the psychologist back safe, if shaken. The fear had made Yvonne vomit, the river bank taking the brunt.

She had missed her, then. She missed her, now.

The DI crossed the room to the sliding doors and peered out over the dunes, remembering the broken Tasha on the beach a few days ago.

Turning the key in the lock, she wandered out onto the soft sand, catching her hair in her hand as it scattered around her head, breathing deep of the sea air and closing her eyes while leaning into the wind, which she could do without falling over.

Yvonne wandered on to where she had found the psychologist on her knees. If asked why she needed to do that, she couldn't have explained it. A compulsion to continue walking until a few feet from the foaming waves. She stayed there for several minutes, turning everything over in her mind, before returning to the relative shelter of the cottage.

Once back, she wandered through to the kitchen where her bag lay on the countertop. No voicemails. One missed call from Dewi. Nothing from Tasha.

She tapped on the missed call from Dewi and waited for him to pick up.

"Hello, Yvonne?"

"Hi, Dewi. I missed a call from you."

"Yes. I thought you should know that we've received a message from the killer."

15

KILLER'S MISSIVE

News crews were everywhere. They had swamped Newtown and the police station car park.

Yvonne sighed, eyes closed and holding her breath, before removing her seatbelt and throwing open the car door.

A reporter pushed a microphone in her face and, as cameras flashed around her, she lost count of the number of times she repeated the phrase, "We're holding a press conference tomorrow. I can't give you more until then, I'm sorry."

Dewi came out of the station to greet her. Give her moral support. He put a hand on her elbow as they pushed inside. "Sorry, about all that. It's gone mad here since we found the second victim and, to make matters worse, the killer sent a letter to the Powys Times, which he wants to go out in tomorrow's print run. The DCI hasn't decided whether to allow them to publish. He's liaising with the crime commissioner and the Home Office and he's asked to speak to you."

"I see." Yvonne ran a hand through her hair. "Where is the letter?"

"It's with the DCI."

"What does it say?"

Dewi shook his head. "So far, only the DCI has seen the message but they know all about it." He flicked his head in the direction of the madness. "At least those at the Powys Times' offices do. Whether they gave that info to other papers is anyone's guess. But the national newspapers and the BBC are aware the killer sent something in, even if they don't have the contents."

"Is it confirmed as coming from the killer?"

"Llewelyn said it mentions the feathers and we haven't released that information. It *has* to be him."

Yvonne took off her coat as she and her sergeant mounted the stairs, throwing it over the back of a chair in CID. "I'd better talk to the DCI and find out what is going on. If I can tell you anything, after we've finished, Dewi, I will."

"Right-oh, ma'am."

∼

YVONNE STRAIGHTENED her skirt and tapped on the DCI's door.

"Come in."

She entered to find him on the phone.

He pointed to a chair next to his desk, running a hand through his hair which appeared unkempt. Not like him at all.

They'd had several meetings since having dinner at his home which she was pleased had passed without awkwardness. She admired the fact he was a gentleman who could take rejection on the chin.

She chewed on the knuckle of her right thumb as she waited for him to come off the phone. From what he was saying, she surmised that he was talking to the crime commissioner, and they were struggling to agree.

"All right. Well, I'll wait for an answer when you've spoken with the Home Secretary." He replaced the phone with a sigh and turned to face her. "Sorry, Yvonne. That was the crime commissioner. You heard about us receiving a letter?"

"Yes, sir, Dewi told me. What's the message?"

He handed her a piece of A4 from his desk, grimacing as he did so. "That's a typed copy. The original is with forensics."

Yvonne read aloud.

"If you go down to the woods today,

you'd better go in disguise.

If you go down to the woods today,

you'll never believe your eyes.

Each protestor, ever there was,

will die in there for certain because?

I'm bored right now and

I'm going to make a picnic.

Hope you like the feathers."

"Sick, huh?"

"Using a child's song, for heaven's sake. Confirms the link between the victim's though."

The DCI nodded. "Campaigners."

"Even more reason to view him as local, wouldn't you say?"

"I would agree." Llewelyn nodded.

"He signed himself Angel of Death." She pursed her lips.

"What's the matter?"

"Nothing." She shook her head. "I came up with that name for him from the beginning, because of the feather he left between the victim's legs."

"Ah, yes, the feathers... Well, the crime commissioner says we should allow the Powys Times to publish this letter, as requested by the killer."

"What will happen if we don't?"

"He doesn't say. He wrote on the envelope, 'to be published in the Powys Times' and he gave tomorrow's date. That means tonight's print run."

"Wow, that doesn't give us much time to decide."

"Exactly. We've got ourselves a killer who wants to play games."

Yvonne remembered Tasha. This was an occasion when her help would have been invaluable. "Are we going send it to print?"

"We are. I'm calling for hunt saboteur and environmentalist groups to join us to discuss safety of their reps out there. We've got a clear target group, and I feel in my bones that the Angel of Death hasn't finished with it, yet."

∼

THE FOLLOWING MORNING, Yvonne found Callum looking through CCTV footage. "Did we get anything useful from Castell-y-Dial?" she asked, as she flicked through her notes for the morning briefing.

"No, ma'am. I'm afraid not. Someone covered it with a plastic bag, most likely the killer. We obtained the bag and forensics have looked it over, but they found no prints and no useful DNA."

"How did the perpetrator reach the camera?"

"Well, it's not that high. There aren't any tall buildings to mount a camera on, so the camera is only five feet up. The owners only had it installed to monitor the entrance. It catches a piece of the road running past and that's about it.

If a vehicle had parked near the entrance they would have caught it with that camera, had the perp left it uncovered."

"And there was only the one camera?"

"Yes."

"That's a pity." Yvonne sighed. "I know people value their privacy, but times like this, you can't have too many cameras, can you?"

Callum nodded. "It's steep up there. It would be tough to carry a person. I think the killer incapacitated Terry Lloyd close to where he died."

"I think so, too. And we know he was protesting the wind farms, so the killer would have known he was likely to be up there. The question is, how is our killer able to isolate his victims. How does he know when they'll be alone?"

"Forums?" Callum asked. "Most campaign groups have a website and social media pages."

Yvonne nodded, her eyes on the trees outside. "And my guess is he would monitor them."

"It would make sense."

"All right. Get the details of all relevant campaign groups in the area, to include their websites and social media pages. Ask Dai to help you. Many groups are closed groups and the killer would have to join them, meaning he would have an identity on their sites. If the same name keeps coming up for the various groups, we should look into it. It's a long shot, but it's worth a go. Concentrate on those people who have joined eco groups over the last twelve months. Keep me up to date."

Callum nodded, stretching to his full height. "Will do."

16

DOUBLE EVENT

The first of June began with a downpour that bounced out of guttering, flooded roads and filled ears with a crescendo of noise.

As Yvonne drove into work, she regretted having taken her wellingtons out of the boot the weekend before, and hoped she wouldn't have to leave the office. It wasn't just the rain. She'd had a fitful night in which sleep had been an elusive and nebulous entity, where death and winged monsters haunted her dreams and cold sweat pervaded her moments awake.

The day seemed wrong. Torn. If anyone had asked her why? She would have struggled to tell them. Something didn't sit right. That was all.

Dewi greeted her as she entered CID. "Leave your coat on, ma'am."

She examined the look on his face, the muscles tense, eyes dark. "What is it, Dewi? What's happened?"

"He struck again. Two victims, this time, in Pen-Yr-Nant wood, near Llanidloes. A male and female, as yet unidentified."

"Oh, no. When?"

"Details are patchy at the moment, but it looks like he attacked the victims some time yesterday and kept them somewhere until he could place them in the wood overnight."

"Damn it!" Yvonne closed her eyes for a second. When she opened them again, they blazed with anger and determination. "All right. Let's get ourselves down there. Find out what happened to them."

She wanted to see for herself and yet dreaded the scene, knowing the killer would have staged it for maximum impact on those attending. Her gut quivered, leaving her feeling sick.

OFFICERS HAD CORDONED off a large part of the wood as teams prepared to comb the surrounding area. The whole of SOCO were on scene. They worked in a numbed silence as they struggled to comprehend the horror before them.

Yvonne and Dewi suited up in the hastily erected tent before going for a closer look at the bodies.

Both victims appeared to be in their twenties. The killer had posed them opposite and facing one another, each propped against a tree, clothed, legs splayed, arms behind them. Hands nailed to their respective trees, just as with previous victims. The male had suffered a nosebleed which had poured over his lips and down his chin. The female had no injury to her face, though her eyes were dark and sunken. Both had the killer's signature, a white swan feather, placed between their legs.

This time, the killer put a rope around the victims' necks and tied them to the trunk, to keep their heads up. To force them to view each other. To watch each other die.

Angel of Death

Yvonne swallowed hard, but the lump in her throat persisted. Every muscle in her body clenched in almost tetanic tightness. Her instinct was to scream with anger, frustration, and horror as those emotions coursed through her, letting her cries echo through the hills and valleys of the surrounding countryside. Instead, she cursed under her breath as tears pricked her eyelids. Her clenched fists blanched as she imagined getting her hands on the person responsible.

A uniformed officer approached the DI as soon as she removed her face mask. "Ma'am?"

"Yes?" She turned to acknowledge him.

"PC Davies." The officer in his forties removed his cap and wiped the sweat from his brow.

"Hello." Yvonne eyed him, head tilted, waiting for him to continue.

"I wanted to inform you that I recognise these victims. We've dealt with them in the past."

Yvonne took out her pocket book. "Go on."

"The male is Robert Griffiths. He works... worked as an apprentice at a local garage. Twenty-five years old and known for being involved in protests in the local area against plans for a leisure complex by Bannerman Holdings. There are a few incidents on PNC. Nothing too serious, but we arrested him for two section five public order offences in the past, in relation to his environmental protests."

"I see. And the female?"

"Sarah Jones, aged twenty-seven and worked in the Red Lion pub in Llanidloes. Again, nothing much on PNC. One section five and a section four public order offence, in relation to protests she carried out. We warned her for pinning up flyers against the proposed leisure complex. She drummed up a lot of support and was a major influence on the local community which got the first planning application for the leisure complex quashed. I understand the second planning application is in and they were protesting it during the last few weeks."

"Thanks for the heads up." Yvonne nodded. "Tell me, were they together?"

"You mean an item?"

"Yeah."

PC Davies shook his head. "As I understand it, they were seeing each other a while back. They shared a flat in Llanidloes. They split up about a year ago and have been living separate lives. I think they only came together for the protests they were both so passionate about."

"Do we have the names of other protesters in their group?"

"I think we filed that information in the system, ma'am. Your guys should be able to access all of that. However, if you need my help, just let me know."

"Thank you, I will."

Dewi rejoined her, after having been to talk with SOCO. "I don't envy them." He flicked his head towards the plastic suits on their knees, swabbing the victims and taking samples. "They were so young."

"I know." Yvonne sighed. "Twenty-five and twenty-seven. No age at all. Their lives had barely begun."

"He planned the whole thing well. Had to have done. Taking down two young people like that. It wouldn't have been easy."

"I agree. And now we know that they were eco warriors, too, confirming our suspicions about the killer's victim choices."

"Them too?" Dewi narrowed his eyes.

Yvonne filled him in with what the PC Davies had said.

"Bannerman Holdings?" Dewi pursed his lips. "Never heard of them."

Yvonne took out her mobile and dialled Callum's number.

"Callum Jones." His voice was firm and even.

"Callum, it's Yvonne."

"Ma'am?"

"Callum, I need you to find out all you can about Bannerman Holdings. Do you remember the brochure that Krysta had in her room? They are the company who would like to build a large leisure complex in the Llanidloes area and have been applying for planning permission. Can you find out who heads the company and, if you can, arrange a meeting with them as soon as possible."

"Will do. Is everything okay out there?"

"No, Callum. We've got a double murder, and the scene is grim."

"Oh, that's not good. Right. I will get on with it, ma'am, and get a meeting set up for you. Do you want me to ring you?"

"No thanks, Callum. I'll catch up with you when we get back to the station."

17

SAFETY FIRST

The meeting room at Newtown library had filled and the noise risen to a level that almost hurt her ears. There was limited seating and several people stood at the margins, arms folded.

Yvonne looked around her. The attendees were angry and frightened. But they were all united in their desire to stop the killer. They wanted police to reassure them that the investigation was progressing and to restore confidence and stability to their community.

Dewi accompanied Yvonne, but the meeting was to be headed up by DCI Llewelyn, who had yet to arrive. She stared at the bare-brick walls of the room, her eyes following the lines of cement from brick-to-brick while she contemplated the murders and closed out the hubbub.

The DCI strode in, peaked cap tucked under his arm, sleeves rolled up, his gaze determined.

That was enough to quiet the room. Within two seconds, the only noise heard was the odd cough and throat-clearing.

"Thanks for coming, everyone," he began. "This has been a difficult time. You have lost friends and colleagues and are living with the fear of being targeted yourselves by a killer who has no conscience. Please let me reassure you that we are doing everything in our power to catch the person or persons responsible and bring them to justice. For now, we need to safeguard you when you are around woodland areas."

Yvonne watched people raise their hands to ask a question, or make suggestions. Llewelyn asked them if they had any idea who would target their community in this way. An uncharacteristic silence greeted him. People looked at each other, hoping they might have the magic answer. Nobody did. And the comments and questions continued.

She watched their expressions, wondering whether anyone in the room could commit the heinous crimes witnessed over the last several weeks. None struck her as a psychopath. That didn't mean they were innocent.

The meeting ran twenty minutes over. But in that time, they agreed an interim plan. Police would be notified when protests were ongoing and would increase patrols in and around woodland, and land under protest. Monitors would be present during land pickets and the DCI would be the main point of contact.

Dates were agreed for followup meetings and community leaders appointed to speak at future press conferences.

As they left, Yvonne felt they had helped assuage the fear in the room, but knew they needed a breakthrough. And soon.

18

FUTURECON

"What do we know about Terry Lloyd?" Yvonne asked her team as they crowded round the Whiteboard in CID.

Callum read from his crib sheet. "Twenty-nine-year-old male, living on Barnfields with his girlfriend Melanie Griffiths who was also an active campaigner in the area. He'd been protesting the siting of wind farms around Mochdre, and destruction of trees he felt to be of historical significance. He wasn't averse to chaining himself to railings and vehicles, in fact."

Yvonne considered for a moment. She knew that wind farms had proliferated over the hills and moors of Mid-Wales over the previous two decades. She tapped her pen against her hand as she spoke. "The proposed wind farm extension at Mochdre would not have surprised the locals. What angered them, was the suggested site, much closer to the town than they had hoped. They worried about the effect it would have on walkers and visitors to the area, the town's own population and some of its historic trees. What does the company do?"

"A Wales-based company, known as Futurecon, it has been in the energy business for the last eighteen years. It started out in the nuclear industry, but over the last decade has moved into the renewable energy sphere."

"Who owns it?"

"A female CEO, name of Serena Wellbrook, forty-four years of age and from Sussex. She lives about an hour from here in Cwm Einion... that is, Artist's Valley."

"That's close to Aberystwyth."

"That's right, it's on the road to Aber from Machynlleth, via Talesin. Anyway, she's quite hands-on and has been down here several times to speak to protesters, herself."

"Okay, well, we should talk to her and to those involved in protesting with Terry. Dai? What's the matter? You're pulling a face."

"Well, ma'am, if we are dealing with a serial killer, then aren't we wasting time talking to locals? I mean, a killer could target the area and not care about any of this. Someone passing through here, a travelling salesman or lorry driver, perhaps."

"Agreed." Yvonne pursed her lips. "But I doubt it and I doubt it is a coincidence that the killer targeted eco warriors. Consider the letter sent in to the Powys Times. Why do that? Why send it to a local paper and not a national paper? A random killer wanting attention would want the maximum attention possible and that would be from the nation. It wouldn't be a warning addressed to local, Welsh environmental protesters. I will stake my reputation on my suspicion that this killer is from the area or connected to the local community and they have a personal issue with eco warriors. The rest is a smokescreen."

Dai folded his arms, unconvinced.

"Look, Dai, come with me. We'll go see Ms Wellbrook

and get her take on what has been happening on her sites. Set the meeting up, would you?"

"Yes, ma'am."

∼

Serena Wellbrook cut an imposing figure, in her double-cuffed, stiff white shirt and grey skirt. Her matching jacket hung on a hook on the right wall of her spacious, light-filled office. The space was an extension to her impressive country home on the side of the spectacular Cwm Einion valley.

Yvonne doubted the CEO had ever wobbled about a decision in her life. Glasses pushed atop her auburn, shoulder-length hair she appeared as though she would brook no argument and visited the gym at least once a week, too, given the biceps which somewhat stretched the material of her blouse. Her face was impeccable, emphasising attractive, strong features.

Yvonne cleared her throat, feeling somewhat dowdy, as Serena showed her to a leather couch, at right angles to the window-wall.

"Can I get you anything?" Serena placed her hands on her hips in a superhero stance.

"Er, no. Thank you."

"Are you sure? I have coffee. It's just percolated." Her voice was as strong as her appearance.

Yvonne put her bag down on the floor, next to her feet. "In that case, yes, I would love a cup. No sugar, thank you."

Serena's heels clicked along the floor to the other side of the office.

Yvonne's gaze wandered the room. Tasteful, oversized prints added interest to the slick, modern furniture her expensive designer had placed exactly so. The room was neat and organised. The DI thought of CID. No comparison.

The shoes clicked-clacked back to her.

"There. One hot coffee and a wafer." Serena smiled. It appeared genuine. She seated herself on the couch, at a forty-five degree angle to Yvonne. "Now, what can I do for you?"

"I came to talk to you about your wind farm sites, near Newtown."

"What about them?"

The DI sipped her coffee, before placing it on a side table next to her. "I understand you've had an issue with ongoing protests against the extension?"

Serena sighed. "Protestors. They get everywhere and with little understanding of what it is they are protesting." She threw the last like daggers.

"They make you angry?"

"Yes, they make me bloody angry. We have to factor in the business risk and costs of those protestors. Do you understand? The permissions will go through anyway, it'll just cost a lot more in time, effort and money. Those protestors cause physical damage to equipment and fencing, not to mention the emotional impact they have upon my staff."

"They believe in what they are doing." Yvonne narrowed her eyes.

"You are aware, Inspector, that our energy plans are environment-friendly?"

"I am aware, just as you are, that that is not the issue, it's where you are siting them which causes..." The DI's voice trailed off.

"You sound as though you agree with them." Serena frowned.

"I'm sorry if that is how it comes across. Let me assure you that I am not picking sides here."

"Conventional, energy production processes are not only worse for the environment, they are a potential target for terror attacks. They can blow pipelines and nuclear plants up, and sabotage them, which would be disastrous for the communities. We have to have alternatives."

"I understand." Yvonne nodded. "I wanted to ask you about the protests at Mochdre."

"What about them?" Serena surveyed the DI with a cool expression in her green eyes.

"We found a young man called Terry Lloyd murdered near a site he had been protesting at."

Serena looked away to the window. "I heard about that."

Yvonne couldn't see the CEO's expression, only the still head, held high. "Did you know him?"

"Not that I am aware. I mean, I have been down there to speak to the protestors myself." She turned to Yvonne. "I don't believe in hiding away. I like to meet adversity head-on. Take the fight to them. Let them know who it is they are dealing with."

"But you don't remember him? I can show you a photograph-"

"No need. His image has been all over the news, along with others, unconnected to any of my sites."

"Do you operate security?"

"I do have security teams who man the sites. We don't man all the sites, but when we do, it is usually one or two guards and maybe dogs. Again, that depends on where the sites are and how much difficulty we expect in keeping them secure."

"CCTV?"

Serena nodded. "We have cameras at many of the sites, but not at Mochdre, I'm afraid."

"Why not?"

"We didn't need them."

"Were guards on duty there?"

Serena shook her head. "Not until we put in the turbines."

"I see."

"There is high metal fencing and billboards, and equipment for digging and heavy lifting. No actual work has started there, yet."

"Do you know of anyone from your company who interacted with Terry Lloyd and would hurt him?"

"No, Inspector."

"And you are sure that you didn't interact with him, yourself?"

"Sure."

Yvonne finished her coffee and picked her bag up from the floor.

Serena sighed. "I am sorry about what happened to that young man. I may get angry at the waste caused by protestors, but I wouldn't dream of hurting one and I am sorry that that young man lost his life, and in such a gruesome way. If I hear of anything, even if it involves members of my staff, I will inform you. Okay? I'm not trying to make your job more difficult."

Yvonne held out her hand. Serena appeared sincere. She liked her. Under different circumstances, perhaps they would be friends. "Thank you for speaking with me."

Serena shook the DI's outstretched hand. "You're welcome."

19

KIM'S HOME TRUTHS

Although the early summer sky was peppered with thicket-like white cloud, the sun stayed out a remarkable percentage of the time. Yvonne checked her watch. Kim would arrive at any moment, excited children at her heels.

She finished gutting fresh trout and washed her hands before checking on the potatoes cooking in the microwave. Yvonne intended making a hot potato salad, with mayo and copious quantities of cracked black pepper. The fresh salad, which she had prepared earlier, sat in the fridge and would only require its lemon and olive oil dressing before serving. A few uncooked sausages and burgers sat in a covered tray next to the barbecue. The utensils were ready. She was ready. She decided not to light it before they arrived, in case something delayed them.

When the car swung into the drive, windows down, music playing, and children singing, Yvonne smiled a broad and heart-felt smile. She couldn't wait to see them.

"Tom! Sally!" She ran towards the vehicle, arms wide.

First Sally, then Tom, asked her to swing them around

Angel of Death

and around. She kissed them both on their foreheads. "My goodness, you have grown, the pair of you." She grinned at them.

"I'm nearly seven." Tom beamed at her.

"Seven? Is that right? Wow. That's so grown-up."

Tom smiled as he and his sister set off around the garden to find treasure.

Yvonne turned her attention to her sister.

Kim had an armful of bags and a bouquet of mixed flowers, which she was trying to hold on to with her teeth.

Yvonne laughed. "Gracious, sis, let me take some of that off you."

"Thanks." Kim said as the DI freed her from the flowers. "They're for you. I hope I haven't squished them too much." Kim put her bags down and smoothed her crumpled, flower-patterned cotton dress, before picking them up again.

"They're beautiful." Yvonne grabbed two of Kim's bags with one hand. "Come on. We'll get these to your rooms and light the barbecue."

∼

"What is it, sis?"

Having eaten most of the food, Yvonne and Kim relaxed back in the garden chairs under the awning, with a glass of wine, while the children played bat-and-ball together.

"What do you mean?" Yvonne took another sip of wine and turned her attention from the hills in the distance to her sister.

"You look preoccupied and a little lost. Sad... I think."

Yvonne grimaced. "Oh, Kim, I'm sorry. I didn't mean to be rude."

"Hey, it's fine. I didn't think you were rude, I was just worried about you. Is something up? Is it a case?"

Yvonne tilted her head. "I *am* working on a difficult and baffling case, but I am trying not to think about it while I have you guys here."

"Are you working on the crucifixion murders?"

"Yes."

"I knew you would be." Kim squeezed her hand. "It's dominating the news. I imagine that's a lot of pressure."

"It is." Yvonne turned her head away, her eyes downcast.

"There's something else." Kim leaned forward in her chair, trying to make eye contact with Yvonne, again. "Yvonne?"

The DI sipped more wine.

"Talk to me." Kim looked across to where her children were playing. They were in their own world and paying no heed.

Yvonne sighed, biting on her lip. "It's Tasha. I'm worried about her."

"Oh?" Kim set down her glass on the table. "What's happened?"

"It's her dad, Kim. He's... he's dying. Pancreatic cancer. It's very advanced, and he is in the final stages. He's in a hospice in Canterbury."

"Oh, gosh. I'm sorry. Poor Tasha."

"I feel like I should be there to support her. If I wasn't working such a difficult case, I would have gone down there by now."

"Well, I'm sure she knows you would be there." Kim rubbed her sister's arm. "She knows what it is like for you."

Yvonne nodded.

"You miss her, don't you?"

Yvonne rubbed her chin, her chest heaved in and out. "I do."

"Did she tell you when she'll be back?"

Yvonne shrugged. "I shouldn't wish for her to come back soon. When she returns, it will be because her father has passed away."

Kim sighed. "I see."

"I've been keeping an eye on her place. It's odd, going there without her."

"You love her, don't you?" Kim's voice was soft.

"What do you mean?" Yvonne asked, her head flicking back to her sister, the colour rising in her cheeks.

Kim reached for her wine glass, her brow furrowed as though searching for the right words. "She loves you. I can tell she does. I've seen you together... Well... I don't think I have ever seen you look so relaxed and happy." Kim's head tilted, eyes flickering as though she were trying to gauge the impact of her words.

"Do you mean happy like I was with David?" Yvonne asked, referring to her late husband.

"Happier." Kim grimaced, as though expecting an admonition from her sister.

Yvonne said nothing, but her body was still as she held her breath.

"She's gay, isn't she? I mean, you've never said, but I can read the signs."

"You don't miss a trick, Kim. Too astute for your own good." Yvonne gave a wry smile

"And she upended her life in London to follow you down here. I mean, that suggests deep friendship... only, I suspected it was more than that."

Yvonne played with the stem of her glass.

"Has she ever said anything to you?"

The DI looked at the ground, running her eyes over the gravel. "She kissed me once."

"I knew it." Kim grinned. "And?"

"And, what?" Yvonne looked up at her.

"What was it like? What did you feel?"

"I don't know." Yvonne shrugged. "I liked it... I guess." She frowned, worried how that might go down.

"You guess?"

"I liked it."

"So, what happened? Did you get cold feet?"

"I'm not-"

"Not what? Gay? Come on, sis. You know I'm not about labels. It doesn't matter what people identify themselves as. It's about what they feel in their heart. You care about people. I'm not surprised that you could fall in love with her. It's always been about the person with you and she *is* a lovely person, and she's very attractive." Kim grinned. "The only reason you haven't confessed to her, is that you haven't yet confessed to yourself. Once you own the words in your mind, you'll be there."

"Does that make me bi-?"

"Who cares? What does it matter? I thought there had to be a reason you walked away from dating your DCI. Especially, after everything you said he had going for him. I thought, hmm, what's going on?"

Yvonne laughed. "Oh, did you?"

"So, what are you going to do now?"

"What do you mean, what am I going to do?"

"What I mean is, are you going to say something to her?"

"No. I can't do that." Yvonne shook her head.

"Why not?"

"I just can't. Anyway, I don't even know if she still feels the same and it would be too much for me to ask her."

"Do you love her?"

Yvonne swallowed. "Yes. Yes, I do." Something burst in her mind, an explosion of absolute clarity. "I think I loved her from the moment I was irritated at her desk appearing in the corner of my office, when I was still in Oxford and I couldn't take my eyes off her. I resented her, but I couldn't help noticing everything: the light in her chocolate hair, the amusement in her dark eyes, the softness of her shirt, and how she was always there, looking out for me. She'd bring me hot soup in a flask if I was out on a late stint. You know, I never considered all of that together, until now."

"Well then, you ought to say something. For the sake of your sanity, if nothing else. Don't let pride stop you from going with your heart, Yvonne. I want so much to see you happy and you've been on your own for far too long."

At that moment, Tom and Sally came running up to them. "Will you come and play ball with us, mummy? Aunty Yvonne?"

Yvonne laughed. "Yes, yes, we will." She flicked her sister an apologetic glance.

"Say something." Kim ordered, before running after her children.

20

SPECTRES

A hint of damp infused the cottage. It followed her from room to room like a cape. She threw open all the windows and allowed the gusty breeze to billow in, breathing deep the smell of boats and nets and fish and holidays.

The sliding door was a little stiff, perhaps in need of oil, as she opened it to access the dunes to the beach. The wind caught her clothing and wrapped her hair around her head as she fought to take the strands out of her mouth and eyes.

In the distance, she saw Tasha alone on the beach, arms outstretched towards the sea, then falling to the sand, her shoulders shaking in violent sobs.

Yvonne ran, sand and wind weighing her down, holding her back, her legs heavy.

"Tasha?" She called out, but the wind caught the words and carried them in the wrong direction.

The grieving woman paid her no heed.

"Tasha?" She threw her arms around the hunched form, but felt only the wind and spray as she fell to the sand.

She looked up and down the beach. No-one there. She

shook her head, tears rolling down her face, fingers digging into the soft, wet sand. And then it changed.

She was running alone through the forest. Searching for a way out. Looking for safety, but instead came across a male and female. Fastened to trees. Limp. Heads fallen forward and blood pouring down their cheeks. Though her gut clenched and her body trembled, she ran to save them, fighting to move her feet; dragging herself forward.

Their heads moved in unison, lifting to stare at her with gaunt faces and blackened eyes. She stopped in her tracks.

"Help us." They screamed in unison, the utterance as terrible as their mouths, which hung open, slack-jawed.

She bolted upright in the dark, shaking, sweat streaming from her. Tears dripping off her chin, her breathing erratic, heart galloping. The clock said four-thirty. It was a nightmare. It wasn't real, and yet it stayed with her.

~

IT WAS STILL with her that evening, when she had continued working for another two hours after the rest of her team had left, going through the events of the last few weeks and perusing photographs, forensic results and vehicle descriptions. Drawing flow charts, writing stuff down, scribbling it out.

She stared into space, trying to make sense of it all.

"You should be at home, Yvonne."

The DI started, heart thudding inside her chest. She hadn't heard the DCI come to the doorway. Why was he still in the building?

She put a hand to her heart to calm it. "You made me jump." She sounded cross, without meaning to.

"Sorry." He grimaced. "That wasn't my intention. You

were miles away. You look tired. What's worrying you, Yvonne? It's not because you are fretting about letting me down, is it? I mean, about seeing me? I'm not offended or upset, honest."

She turned to him, noting the concern in his eyes, and sighed. At that moment, she thought she might tell him of her concern for Tasha, and how much she missed her, and that this case was getting under her skin. But she refrained, keeping her thoughts in a secret place. Believing that, even if she disclosed everything, he wouldn't be able to help her, anyway.

"No, no. I mean, it's not that I'm not sorry about not being ready to date. I like you, just not in... not..."

He held up his hand. "It's okay. I should know better, anyway, in my position. I don't think for one minute that the Super would have approved." He grinned. "We would have gotten into a lot of hot water."

She smiled back at him. "You are a good man, Chris. You will make someone an amazing husband."

"Gee, thanks."

"You know what I mean."

"Get your coat," he ordered. "You're going home."

21

JAKE BANNERMAN

Yvonne discarded her jacket over the back of her chair, before grabbing a coffee and heading to find Callum and Dai.

"Did you get anything on Bannerman Holdings?" she asked, undoing the cuffs on her blouse and rolling her sleeves up to just below the elbows.

Callum handed her a small file with the notes he had printed off. "Over the last ten years, Bannerman Holdings have gained swathes of land across the UK, which they are developing or looking to develop, and for which they are seeking developmental planning permissions. Some sites were brown field. Others, like the one near Llanidloes, are common greenfield sites and beauty spots."

"You say gained?" Yvonne frowned. "Have they bought the site near Llanidloes, then?"

"Well, that's the strange thing. Final negotiations for the sale are ongoing, but the current owners applied for the first lot of planning permissions on Bannerman Holdings' behalf. Jake Bannerman insisted that planning permission must be in place before his company would purchase the land."

"I heard they turned the first lot of planning down?" Yvonne flicked through the pages Callum had given her.

"That's right, they did. The protesters were vocal at the various meetings and drummed up a lot of support for their cause within the local community. They use the land in question to walk their dogs and take their children for picnics, etc. There would be some disruption to wildlife, also a factor."

"So, now they are applying for planning permission, again?"

"Right, but it looks like the new permission is being sought by Bannerman Holdings, themselves, as they feel they would be better at getting it through."

"Can they do that before the sale?"

"As long as the current owner's signature is also on the paperwork, yes. It just means that Bannerman Holdings will be out-of-pocket by the planning costs, if their pitch is unsuccessful. My guess is, if they lose again, they'll move on."

"What do we know about Jake Bannerman?"

"He's in the area, for meetings with Powys Council. He's staying in Montgomery. I've got you half an hour with him at the Dragon Hotel in Monty, tomorrow at half-eleven. His secretary said he'll be happy to answer questions." Callum pulled a face. "Very generous of him, I'm sure."

"Thank you, Callum and Dai. Good work, both of you." She grinned at them. "I can't wait to meet him." Her lip curled in sarcasm.

THE DRAGON HOTEL in Montgomery impressed her. Built in the 17th-century as a coaching inn, it had a period black-and-white front. The rooms had exposed beams and contained many of the original features from the Elizabethan era. Yvonne could understand why it was popular with wealthy visitors to the area.

Jake Bannerman agreed to see her in his suite.

She went alone as the rest of her team were busy gathering information around Bannerman Holdings and Futurecon. Callum had discovered that Terry Lloyd was protesting against both companies at the time he lost his life.

A member of staff showed her to Bannerman's room. She took a deep breath, before knocking on the substantial door.

"Come in."

It reminded her of entering the DCI's office and she had a similar sense of trepidation as she always had when knocking on Llewelyn's door, as though she might be in for a ticking off. She gave herself a mental shake and went in.

Jake Bannerman did not rise. He sat on a sofa, dressed in suit trousers and shirt, a loose red tie draped around his neck. His grey eyes observed her without expression, as though he was weighing her up without wanting to give anything of himself away. His blonde hair was short and styled with a trendy quiff. He appeared to be someone who kept a tight control of his image.

Yvonne estimated him to be around forty years of age. "Thank you for agreeing to this meeting," she said, in the most confident voice she could muster, walking up to him whilst holding out her hand.

He accepted it with a firm shake which he twisted somewhat, so he had the upper hand.

Yvonne removed hers.

"I must admit, it surprised me to hear I was having a visit from the police. What can I help you with, Inspector?"

Although not invited, Yvonne took a seat on the chair at right angles to him, removing her bag and coat. "Mr Bannerman, I don't know if you are aware, but we've had a double murder on some land in which you have a vested interest."

He stared at her and she could tell from the flickering of his eyes, that he was calculating his answer. Did he think she was trying to trap him? Or, something else?

"I was aware. I learned about it first thing this morning." He leaned back on the sofa and folded his arms. "Am I a suspect, given that the people killed were protesting my proposed use of the land?"

"You are a person of interest, Mr Bannerman." Yvonne kept her tone cool and even. "Suspect might be too strong a word, though you may have information that could be relevant."

"How so?"

"I understand that you, yourself, visited a picket a few weeks ago, back on the fourth of May. Am I right?" She watched for any change in his demeanour. There was none.

He appeared controlled. Face and body. "That's right. I wanted to see it for myself. It was a civil affair. Bit of shouting from the opposite side, but no arrests."

"The council must have disappointed you when they turned your first lot of planning permission down."

"Well, yes they did." He brushed a hand across his knee twice. "But I'm used to the cut and thrust of such negotiations. They're par for the course. I don't see it as an incitement to murder, if that is what you're thinking."

"Do you have security at your sites, Mr Bannerman?"

"Jake, please," he said, but there was no warmth in it.

"Jake." She added, but it gave her no pleasure to use his first name.

"We use security when we are expecting a major protest. The protestors always claim that they are the environmentally conscious ones, which you wouldn't think, given the damage we sometimes encounter and have to deal with."

"Did the protestors on the Mochdre site cause damage, then?"

"Well, they removed barriers and a billboard which showed the proposed layout of the leisure complex. They left them lying in a field."

"I see." So no major damage, she thought.

"A lot of work and financial investment goes into these plans. We rework and redraw plans many times, before they go to the councils for planning permission. We aim to be environmentally friendly and sensitive and we hash out whatever issues we can foresee. I don't want to rub up against the local community. I want them on board. On my side. My sites provide jobs, growth, and pleasure for those not hell-bent on having a lean-to for the hell-of-it."

"I'm not picking sides." Yvonne pursed her lips. "But I understand it concerned the protestors that wildlife would suffer and the complex would be inaccessible to locals who might wish to walk on the land and that they would have to pay as opposed to walking for free, which they do now."

"Well, any development would be likely to enclose land which would then become private. As for the wildlife, it would be disrupted for one year. An extensive lake within the proposal would bring further wildlife into the area." He looked self-satisfied with the last, placing both hands behind his head, puffing his chest out.

"Did you ever speak with Robert Griffiths or Sarah Jones?"

"Who?" His brow furrowed.

"A young couple murdered on the land. Crucified, actually."

"Oh, God." He jerked his head back. "Extreme way to go."

"It was horrific."

"If I did, I don't remember."

Yvonne reached into her handbag and produced a recent photograph, given to her by Robert's family. It showed him grinning at the camera, as he was mid air in a snow-covered scene, somewhere in the Alps.

She showed it to Bannerman. "That's Robert Griffiths. Full of life. He enjoyed snowboarding. His loss has devastated his parents."

"I don't remember speaking to him. Someone from my security team may have, if he was protesting at the site."

"Do you use your own security? Or is it contracted in?"

"Contracted. Aside from my personal protection. I've had the same close-protection team for the best part of ten years. They're superb. You can't be too careful these days."

"But you contract in for the site?"

"Yes."

"How well do you know the firm you use under the contract?"

"G-Force? Well, Inspector. They have an impeccable reputation in the field. They excel at what they do, are reliable, and they do a professional job for a reasonable fee. What's not to like?"

"They've had one or two run-ins with locals before, though, haven't they? Didn't a protester have a heart attack after being pushed on his back by one of G-Force's security guards last year?"

"I don't recall."

"It made national news."

"I don't read the papers."

"On the telly."

"Oh."

"And there were some rather unsavoury incidents at a private prison during the year before, if I remember correctly."

Bannerman shrugged.

"Signing a multi-million pound contract for an hotel and leisure complex is a good motive for murder, wouldn't you say?"

"So, I am on the suspect list? A minute ago, you said I was only a person of interest?"

"I'm just trying to get my head around it all, Mr Bannerman."

"Okay, well, I didn't kill that couple and, as far as I am aware, neither did anyone who works for me, contracted or not."

Yvonne sighed. "Okay." She reached into her bag to retrieve one of her cards. "Here is my number. If you hear anything that might interest us, be sure and let me know. I'll let myself out."

22

TASHA'S RETURN

Although reluctant, Tasha agreed to stay with Yvonne for several days, following her father's death.

"You shouldn't be alone at a time like this." Yvonne had told her down the phone, being unable to bear the thought of Tasha being isolated after her bereavement. She could still see the psychologist on her knees on the beach outside her home and the image cut her to the quick.

"Well, I would enjoy your company and your sensible head." Tasha sniffed. "I just don't want to be a burden."

"You are never a burden, Tasha. How's your mum? How's she taking it all?"

"She took it hard. She has gone to stay with her brother and his wife for a few weeks and we'll explore how she is after that. It's possible she'll come to stay at my cottage, if she's not any better about things."

"Good. That's good. Well then, I'll greet you when you get here."

"Good."

"Bye, then." Yvonne pulled a face as she finished the call. Words were harder, now that she had recognised her feelings for Tasha. Things which had been easy, now seemed difficult beyond measure. She needed to see her and yet the nerves made her sick. The DI wondered how she would deal with that, let alone put what she was experiencing into words. And yet, everything and everywhere she looked had a fresh and vibrant brilliance, like it had only just sprung into existence, newly born from some giant womb.

∼

Tasha arrived lugging a suitcase and a large holdall. Yvonne met her at Newtown rail station, rubbing her palms down the sides of her skirt as she ran forward to help.

The psychologist dropped the suitcase and bag and held her arms out for a hug which Yvonne gave, holding on for a little longer than was usual.

"Are you all right?" she asked, as she pulled away from Tasha to examine the puffiness below her eyes and the weight loss, evidenced by hollowed cheeks. She squeezed her arm before grabbing the holdall to take it to the car.

"I'm getting there." Tasha trundled the suitcase behind the DI.

"I'm so sorry for your loss." It seemed inadequate, but Yvonne struggled for the right words.

"Hey, it's okay. It's my mum I'm worried about. She has hardly slept since... since-"

"I know." Yvonne gave her a knowing look. "Thank goodness she has somewhere to go."

"Yes."

They lifted the baggage into Yvonne's car and the DI

adjusted the positioning, so she could close the boot. "Have you eaten?" She asked, moving round to open the passenger door for Tasha.

"Not yet." Tasha gazed at her, a question in those dark brown eyes.

The DI turned her head away, quickly moving round to the driver's side.

They drove most of the way to Yvonne's home in silence. Several times, she thought she should break it and yet the words still would not come. She felt tongue-tied and lacking, even though there were so many thoughts swirling in her head. Things welling inside of her, wanting to burst forth.

～

THE SUN WAS SETTING as they pulled into Yvonne's drive, shedding a russet glow over the trees and the house. The temperature had dropped a little, and the DI resolved to light a fire while she prepared something tasty to eat. Something that would happily cook in the oven while they shared a glass or two and talked.

"Is it all right if I shower?" Tasha asked, before taking the bags through to her room.

"Yes, it is. You don't have to ask." Yvonne tucked a stray lock of hair behind her ear. "I'll get a fire and some food started." She smiled. "I'll see you soon."

The fire spat and crackled as it got going enough for Yvonne to leave it be and start dinner. She decided that tuna lasagne and garlic bread would be the way to go. Easy to make and fortifying as she was sure Tasha was not eating properly.

With the food in the oven, she poured two ample glasses of red wine and headed back to the lounge, feeding the fire with another couple of logs. Tasha was not yet back.

Yvonne looked about and took several large cushions from the sofa, arranging them on the floor so that they might sit in front of the fire, with their wine, in comfort. A twinge of doubt had her picking them back up and placing them back on the sofa before once again changing her mind and placing them back on the floor, rearranging them again for good measure.

Fighting the nerves, she gulped some of her drink.

"Oh my, get this." Tasha's smile lit her face, as she entered the lounge and saw the fire, the full glasses, and the arranged seating on the floor. "I'm being very taken care of." The question was back in her eyes as she studied the DI's face.

"Here's your wine," Yvonne blurted, as she handed her a glass. "I'm just going to check on the food." She was running away, but couldn't help herself. She needed to find the right moment and was scared she might time it wrong. Running was easier.

When she returned, Tasha sat amongst the cushions, sipping her drink and staring into the flames. Yvonne could tell the psychologist was concentrating and took her seat, so as not to disturb whatever thoughts her friend was pondering. The smell from the kitchen tantalised her nostrils.

Tasha turned to her, as though realising she had been miles away and wanting to make amends. "And how are you? What's happened in your world since I went away?"

Yvonne cleared her throat, looking back towards the flames. "I'm well, thank you. I've been busy at work, and worried about you."

There was a warmth about Tasha's smile, accompanied as it was by the tenderness in her eyes.

Yvonne brushed her tongue over her lip. "Actually," she blurted as a fragile thread of confidence gave her a push, "there's something I wanted to tell you..." Her voice trailed away, as another wave of sickness knotted her stomach.

"What?" Tasha tilted her head, concerned.

"Well, I..."

"Yvonne? What is it?"

"We're hunting another crazy killer." The words were rushed and wrong and a million miles from what she intended. She closed her eyes, inwardly cursing herself.

"Oh, no. Not another one." Tasha leaned in, trying to read Yvonne's thoughts. "Do you want to talk about it?"

No, Yvonne thought. *That is the last thing I want.* "I'm not sure."

"Would you like my help?"

"No, I mean, I shouldn't impose on you. You have been through so much. I don't even know why I needed to mention it."

"Well, it's weighing you down and if I can help, I will. It's the least I can do."

"You're an amazing person and a wonderful friend."

Tasha laughed. "Likewise."

After further prodding, Yvonne filled Tasha in on the case, their conversation continuing through dinner, while seated at the table.

"Would you like me to construct a profile?" Tasha asked between mouthfuls.

"I'll speak with the DCI." Yvonne nodded. "He mentioned the possibility of us getting a profile done, and I'm sure he will agree to you having another consultancy role with us. I don't see how he could refuse."

"Can I view the case notes?"

"I should think so. I'll sort it. You can visit the incident room. Come in with me, tomorrow."

Tasha smiled. "It's a date."

23

TROUBLE AT THE FARM

"What are you doing, letting those kids on my land again?" Emmanuel Tunicliffe strode up to his gamekeeper, Trevor Tindall and glared at him.

They were standing outside Tindall's two-bed cottage on the edge of the forest.

Trevor swallowed hard. "Well, I didn't think they were doing any harm-"

"I found two carrier bags full of rubbish, left hanging on a gatepost at the edge of the wood."

"Well, perhaps they meant to take them, but forgot. They cleared everything else away."

"Look, it's your job to see that they do not abuse my property or disturb the animals. It looks to me like you've been slacking. And, anyway, what were they protesting this time?"

"The pheasant shoot, sir."

"What? Is that why half my stock was found wandering the roads? I had the RSPCA ringing the other day, telling me that too many of my birds are ending up dead on the highways and I keep being reported by concerned motorists and walkers."

"Well, I-"

"Do your job, Tindall. It's what I pay you for."

"I can't make them leave."

"You can call the police. God, threaten them with the shotgun, if you have to. Anything. Just keep them out." Tunicliffe scowled. "You let this continue and I'll dock your wages."

"That's not fair. There's only one of me."

"You're a fit man, Tindall and that scowl on your face is enough to scare anyone."

Tindall rubbed his forehead. "I'll do my best, sir."

"Oh, and take the Land Rover into the garage, will you? It's got a flat tyre."

Tindall eyed his employer, his forehead furrowed. "How did that happen?"

"I don't know. Get it to the garage, will you? Tell them I'll pay when I collect."

"Right." Tindall scratched his stubble.

"Some time today would be good."

24

EVA

Eva Wilde split from the main group, heading for the pheasants, intending to give them freedom. She held a pair of wire-cutters and a thick glove, for this purpose, plus a jacket to throw over the CCTV camera. She waited for it to be dark enough to act.

The noises in the forest grew more eerie as night drew in. An owl hooted nearby, and she hoped Ed and his friend Matt would create a diversion on the opposite side of the land, making it easier for her to get the job done.

A crunching came from somewhere behind and her heart lurched in her chest. Breathing heavily, she cowered, turning her head towards the direction the noise came from. It sounded like someone's stepping on branches or brush. There were further sounds, someone walking in the forest. They were moving away from her. She rose from her position, peering in the direction she thought the person had gone, but saw nothing and no-one.

She walked about ten yards along and found a mallet leaning against a tree and lifted it with both hands. It was heavy with a large metal head. Too heavy for her to use.

Angel of Death

The footsteps were on their way back.

Still with the mallet in her hands, she backtracked to her original hiding place, in a dry stream bed, tucked under a fallen tree, and lay the mallet beside her. In the distance, she could see the beam of a torch sweeping the brush and hoped that Ed and Matt would create the diversion, soon or she could do nothing about the pheasants.

The sweeps of the torch beam continued for at least another fifteen minutes, while the night grew colder. She used the spare jacket as a kind of blanket to protect her from the worst of the chill, relieved when the carrier of the torch appeared to head off to another part of the wood.

There was no sign of a diversion. The footsteps came again. She thought about Krysta and the others who had died. She prayed she had hidden the mallet well enough. Though police were tight-lipped regarding the manner of the deaths, rumours had spread that someone had used a mallet to bring the victims under control.

And now, he stood at the tree where the mallet had been, his torch beam searching the undergrowth. He hesitated now, appearing jumpy, realising he wasn't alone and her heart thudded as she inhaled a deep breath, to quiet her breathing, before he turned and moved away.

She heard the engine of a truck start up and exhaled with a sigh. She waited a further five minutes before moving closer to the pheasants. In the distance, shouts went up. Her cue. Ed and Matt were creating the diversion.

25

KILLER PROFILED

Tasha poured over the documents and photographs of heart-rending scenes, all too vivid on the high-definition images.

"He takes a real pleasure in watching them deteriorate, doesn't he? I mean, it would take hours for them to die." Tasha pursed her lips.

"Do you think he watches them the whole time?" Yvonne frowned.

"From a safe space? Yes, I do. Otherwise, why kill them like this? Why not give a fatal blow to the head with the mallet instead of incapacitating them? Oh no, he wants them to wake up. He needs them to realise the hopelessness of their situation, and that they will die and there is nothing they can do about that. The suffering is everything to him. He hates them and what they stand for."

"Do you think he's deranged?"

"If you're asking if there is evidence of psychopathy, the answer is yes. Whether he wants it to look that way, to cover his tracks, is another question. We won't know which category he fits into, until you catch him and we get him under analysis and observation."

"Hmm. How old do you think he is?"

"Given the crime and his level of confidence? I'd say somewhere in the thirty-five to fifty-five age range."

Yvonne nodded.

"Tell me about your suspects. Do you have people that age?"

Yvonne grimaced. "Most of our suspects would fall into that category and one or two would fall just outside."

"Oh." Tasha rubbed her cheek. "Not to worry. Other traits should narrow it down for you."

"Okay, fire away." Yvonne's eyes wandered over Tasha's face, and her long eyelashes, while the psychologist read from the notes in front of her.

"The killer is an intelligent male with a super-ego who fears that his intelligence and superiority is going unrecognised by those around him. He will exhibit ritualistic behaviours, like OCD and get up in the small hours, while everyone he knows is still sleeping. And he'll get kicks from that, like he's better than them because of it. He may live alone, but, if he doesn't, his closest family will know the rituals, such as excessive tidiness, hand washing or similar. I expect him to be fit and he'll take regular exercise. Again, he will most likely have a rigid system with an obsessive quality to it. He collects feathers. This may also be an obsession and someone is likely to have noticed them around his home, or boxes or bags of feathers in a room in his house or in a shed. He has some claim to the land where he murdered his victims, though this claim may be imaginary. Maybe his family have historical ties to it, or he owns it."

"Is he targeting specific victims?"

"He will have come up against his victims at some point,

in the form of personal arguments with them or with the groups they represent. The murders are personal, a revenge of sorts. He's taking a keen interest in your investigation, the letter shows that. He will follow newspaper articles, reading anything that can tell him what you are up to and how close you might be to catching him. He will keep handing you nuggets designed to mislead, so beware of any letters. Also, let none of your officers go anywhere on their own while they are investigating this case."

Yvonne frowned. "Will he target one of us?"

"It's unlikely, but it is possible, since he has communicated with you, via the letter to the press. And you've been there before, Yvonne. You, better than anyone, should realise what this sort of killer is capable of."

The DI sighed. "Yes, that is true."

"That is the meat of my profile, Yvonne. I will get it typed out and copied ready for your briefing, tomorrow. I hope it helps you." Tasha turned, giving her a broad smile.

Yvonne's heart jumped, pumping like it was supplying blood to the whole office. She bit her lip, holding her breath. Perhaps, now was the moment. The time to disclose what she was holding inside.

She moved her chair back, so that she could face the psychologist. "I would like say something, Tasha. Something that-"

A loud knock made them start and Callum burst in. "Sorry to disturb you, ma'am, but you'll want to hear this."

Yvonne pushed her chair away from Tasha's, her eyes wide and staring, heart thumping. "Right... err, what is it, Callum?"

"A lad called Matt Talbot has just come into the station with information regarding Bannerman holdings and an altercation that happened between Jake Bannerman and

Robert Griffiths."

"Robert Griffiths?" Callum had her full attention. "As in, the male victim of the double murder?"

"That's the one."

Yvonne looked at Tasha. "I'm sorry, I'd better go. Come with me, if you'd like?"

Tasha nodded. "I'd like to, thanks."

∽

MATT TALBOT WAITED for them in interview room one, wearing a loose linen shirt and shell necklace, his dark hair in a ponytail. The date of birth he had given at the front desk, would make him twenty-nine. She noted the sheen of sweat on his forehead and the way he curled the fingers of one hand around those of the other, on the desk in front of her. She felt for him, her empathy only increased because both his eyelids drooped down to halfway, and he had to tilt his head back to look at her.

"Thank you for coming in to speak with us, Matt. I understand you have some information you think might help our enquiry?"

He nodded. "I- I- I do."

She noted the stutter, but did not remark upon it. She cast a glance at Tasha before proceeding. "I'm sorry to ask you this, but are you okay? Is there something wrong with your eyes?"

"M- M- Myasthaenia Gravis," he blurted.

"Sorry, I don't-"

"It's au- autoimmune disease. It affects my m- m- muscles."

"I see. I'm sorry to hear that."

He shook his head. "It's o- okay."

"How long have you had that, Matt?"

"S- since I was a t- teenager." He continued to hold his hands as though to stop them shaking.

"Did you know Robert Griffiths well?"

He nodded. "Qu- quite well. I knew him since high school."

"What happened with Jake Bannerman? I understand there was an argument?"

"Y- yes, there was. W- we were p- protesting at a site near Llani."

"Llani? You mean Llanidloes?"

"Y- yes. We'd been there for a w- week, or two."

"Okay."

"Bannerman w- wants to build a paid leisure park on the l- land and the c- community are dead-against it."

"So, what happened?"

"B- Bannerman came to meet with surveyors. W- we wouldn't let him enter. R- Rob stood in front of him and w- wouldn't let him pass."

"What happened next?"

"Bannerman pushed him. R- Rob fell backwards. When he got up, he p- pushed Bannerman right back. I th- thought he would hit him, but he j- just held the placard up to Bannerman's f- face."

"Bannerman g- grabbed the board and smashed it on the g- ground. They were shouting and sw- sw- swearing at each other."

"Did Bannerman call the police?"

"N- no. s- security guards came. Bannerman's p- people."

"Did they break it up?"

"Th- they moved us further back and parked vehicles in the g- gateway to stop us from going back."

Angel of Death

"Bannerman th- threatened Rob. He said he'd be waiting for him when he least expected it."

"Did he? Wow."

"I- I thought you should kn- know that."

"It's helpful. Thank you, Matt."

"Rob was a good p- person. He didn't deserve wh- what happened to him."

Yvonne nodded. "I know. No-one deserves to die like that. Can I ask you, are you still doing protests on the land?"

Matt nodded, looking down at his hands.

"For your own safety, and for the sake of our investigation, I would urge you not to until we catch the killer."

"O- okay."

"We may need to speak to you again, Matt. Where can we reach you?"

Matt took out a mobile phone from his pocket and switched it on. "I- I can give you my n- number."

"Okay, great."

As Matt left, Yvonne turned to Callum and Tasha. "I think we should pay Mr Bannerman another little visit."

26

CAPTURE

Something struck Eva from behind. She didn't see it coming. After the truck engine died away, and the shouts from Ed and Matt went up, she believed it safe to approach the poultry pens and was in the middle of cutting the fence, not hearing the footsteps approach. As she fell, a hand grabbed her hair, tugging her backwards until her head throbbed and her legs shook. She cried as he hit her on the side of the head with a wooden bat. Her attacker made no sound. Pain seared through her head and neck and blood clouded the vision in her right eye. She fainted.

When she came too, blindfolded, gagged and hog-tied, she lay on the cold metal flooring of a vehicle which bounced over humps in the ground, aggravating her injuries. She lifted her head to protect it and to listen for any other sound other than the engine and the bumping of the wheels, but could hear nothing else. They were off-roading, and the ride was torturous.

The gag muffled her cries as tears flowed down her cheeks. She prayed that Ed and Matt would realise what

Angel of Death

happened and alert the police. If they didn't, the police wouldn't find her in time.

She wet herself, unable to hold her urine any longer. This added to her misery as the initial warmth gave way to a cold which travelled the length of her. She closed her eyes and continued to pray.

~

YVONNE WAS in the office alone, the team having left for home and Tasha having headed to the cottage to receive a delivery from an electrical company.

She thought back to earlier in the day, and how close she came to confessing her feelings to the psychologist, before Matt Talbot interrupted them. Perhaps, she mused, fate intervened to stop her disclosing anything she might regret, or had decided the timing was wrong. She remembered the question in Tasha's eyes and how Dewi and Callum's presence meant the psychologist never voiced it. It hung in the air, cloaking the DI as she returned to work.

As though a supernatural message passed between them, Yvonne's mobile buzzed, informing her of the arrival of a text. She reached into her jacket pocket and retrieved the phone, knowing in her bones it would be from Tasha even before she looked at the screen. It was. Two words. 'Call me.'

She knew the psychologist wanted to hear what was going on inside her head, but Yvonne couldn't send her feelings by text or voice them down a phone. She would say what she felt while looking into Tasha's eyes. Eyes, whose expression she could read and confirm, at once, the truth of the matter, and whether Tasha shared her feelings as she hoped she did. For this reason, she did not return her friend's call.

In the meantime, spread on the desk and on her open laptop, were the notes and timelines that they had scraped together regarding the suspects. Top of the list were both Bannerman and Tunicliffe.

Bannerman was in the right age group, with bucket loads of confidence and a claim over the land on which they found two bodies and he appeared to have a super ego. She could envisage him having a large collection of feathers, although they had no information to suggest that he did. He'd also had a major argument with one victim, that had become physical, and he appeared to want to take it further.

Tunicliffe was the right age, too. He lived alone and owned land in which they had found some of the victims. He was muscular and appeared to have a sizeable ego. She would speak to Tindall again, to find out what he knew as regards Tunicliffe's character.

Neither Bannerman nor Tunicliffe had a police record, so the PNC check was fruitless. She wondered whether either of the prime suspects collected feathers, or suffered with visual impairment or OCD. That is why she had stayed late, to trawl the web for information on Bannerman, anything in the public domain. She had spent two hours going through everything, but could find no evidence of OCD or obsessive collecting. Their only other option was to speak to friends and colleagues and perhaps re-interview Bannerman.

She wrapped up in the office by writing herself a few notes ready for the morning, prioritising what they needed to know as soon as possible. Following that, she grabbed her coat and left, reading her text from Tasha one more time before placing the phone in her bag and closing the clasp.

The air outside was cool enough that she raised the collar on her jacket on her way to her car. The blackbirds sang their evening song, and the wind wrapped her skirt around her legs. She hoped the Angel of Death would refrain from attacking anyone that night.

27

TERROR

"So, come on, what was it you wanted to tell me?" Tasha stood behind Yvonne as the DI poured coffees for the team. "I sent you a text last night. Didn't you get it?"

Yvonne cleared her throat, her back muscles tensing. "Yes, I got it..." Her voice trailed away as she stirred sugar into Dewi's tea. "I couldn't phone you last night. I was up to my ears in it and was here until stupid o'clock trying to wade through all the pieces of information we've gathered, researching Bannerman." She turned, her eyes falling on Tasha's soft cotton blouse.

Tasha tilted her head, placing a hand on Yvonne's arm, her voice soft. "What did you want to tell me? It seemed important."

"Well, I-"

Dewi shouted to her. "Ma'am?"

"Oh, for crying out loud," Yvonne muttered under her breath, gritting her teeth in frustration. "I'm sorry, Tasha. It *is* important. I will speak to you later, in person, and not on the phone. Maybe we can get tea somewhere? The Bank Tearooms, perhaps?"

"Sure." Tasha nodded, her face muscles tense. She took a moment to step back and allow the DI past. "Let's do that."

∽

"What is it Dewi? You sound out of breath."

"I am, ma'am. Eva Wilde's father has informed us that Eva is missing. He is downstairs completing a missing person's report as she hasn't seen her since the night before last."

"What? She's been missing over twenty-four hours? Why are we only finding out now?"

Dewi shrugged. "Mr Wilde said he only found out this morning."

"Who told him?"

"Ed."

"Come on." Yvonne headed for the stairs, knocking over a chair in the process. "Let's get down there. I want to speak to him before he leaves."

Dewi replaced the fallen chair and followed her down.

"Mr Wilde?"

"Yes. Tom Wilde." The gentleman with cropped grey hair turned to greet her, his face creased, eyes dark.

"I'm sorry to hear that Eva is missing." Yvonne pursed her lips. "When did you last see her?"

Tom Wilde rubbed the back of his head. "Well, it would have been about four days ago. She came for supper with myself and her mum and we chatted for about an hour."

"How was she, when you spoke with her?"

"Fine. She was the same as usual." He paused, his eyes

glazed. "I mean, she was moaning about things that were happening in the community, but only the usual stuff. We were used to her caring so much about things. I suspect she will turn up today or tomorrow, but... but with what's been happening-"

"You mean the murders?"

"Right." His eyes widened. "I don't want to take chances."

"How did you find out that your daughter was missing, Tom?"

"Ed Lawton said she had been with them the night before last, at the poultry pens, back of Ryde Hall Farm."

"What were they doing there?" The DI's eyes narrowed.

"Well, according to Ed, Eva was intent on setting the young pheasants free. Said they were so distressed, Tunicliffe had fitted them with face masks to stop them pecking each other to death. Ms Wilde witnessed several females with missing back feathers. Ed and Matt were to create a diversion while she cut the metal fencing with wire cutters."

"Okay, Tom, thank you. Finish filing the details and I will speak to Ed and find out what he knows about that night." She turned to her DS. "Dewi? Can you take Callum or Dai and get over to Ryde Hall? Get a backup unit to go with you and get the DCI's permission to have an armed response vehicle on standby. As soon as I have spoken with Ed Lawton, I will join you, okay?"

"Will do. Are you going to speak to Ed on your own?"

"I'll take Tasha."

"Right-oh. I'll see you when you join us."

~

EVA ESTIMATED that it had been over twenty-four hours since she last ate. She was cold, hungry and tired, but sleep, when she snatched some, was fitful, sporadic and spawned from exhaustion more than restfulness. Hog-tied and blindfolded, every part of her hurt. Even shifting position brought little relief.

Having not seen the person who abducted her, she still did not know his identity, only that his hands were rough as he threw her from the vehicle. She was in a building somewhere. She passed out during the journey and had no way to measure time. Daylight filtered through the blindfold as he ejected her from the truck.

A door creaked open, and footsteps followed behind her. Rough hands removed the gag from her mouth and a sandwich was placed in its stead. A knee, pressed on her uppermost elbow, preventing her from turning towards her abductor. Hungry, she took a bite out of the sandwich.

"Hello?" she said, after eating several mouthfuls and drinking a few gulps from a water bottle held to her face. "Who are you? Why are you doing this? Can I go, now? I'm sorry about the pheasants. Hello?"

He replaced the gag, the footsteps receding until the door closed after him.

"Wait, I need the toilet." The words were a muffled nonsense, and he had left, anyway. Hot tears raced down her cheeks.

28

SOMETHING SHADY

Trevor Tindall parked the pickup next to the sheds before jumping down to get his lunch box. As he crossed the yard, he saw Emmanuel Tunicliffe coming out of the end barn and locking it with a padlock. Having walked a couple of steps, Tunicliffe returned to give the padlock a further tug.

"All right, sir?" The gamekeeper called, his eyes narrowing.

Tunicliffe appeared not to hear him.

"I thought I'd have my lunch, now," Tindall continued, eyeing the locked doors.

Tunicliffe finally registered Tindall's presence. "Trevor. Where did you come from?" His gaze flicked around, taking in the pickup and Tindall's muddy boots.

"I've been out checking on the sheep. A motorist popped by the cottage to let me know several of the lambs had escaped and gotten onto the road, sir. Found them all and put them back and I've made a temporary repair on the fencing. I must get a more permanent repair sorted, after I've eaten, or they'll get through again."

"More vandalism." Tunicliffe frowned. "Check on the pheasants, when you've finished, will you? There's damage to that fencing, too. Damned protestors again, no doubt."

Tindall nodded. "I'll get on to it, sir."

With that, Tunicliffe left. Heading for the main house, Tindall presumed.

∽

YVONNE PUT HER FOOT DOWN, only just staying the right side of the speed limit. It was times like this, she wished she had easy access to a marked vehicle.

She sensed the tension in Tasha and, although questions hung over them like a pall, she lacked the time to address them now. Eva Wilde was missing. That had to take priority.

"God, I hope he doesn't have her. For all we know, he may have crucified her already." Yvonne paused at the traffic lights, cursing under her breath and tapping the steering wheel with her thumbs.

"How far are we from her boyfriend's place?" Tasha asked, without turning round.

"About ten minutes. He's expecting us, so we should be able to speak with him as soon as we arrive. With any luck, he'll take us to her last known whereabouts.

"Didn't you say she was last seen heading for the poultry pens at Ryde Hall?"

"I did, but she may not have made it that far. If Ed shows us where she was in the wood when they split up, SOCO can trace her from there."

"Is there any chance she went into hiding?" Tasha pointed to the lights which had changed.

Yvonne put her foot down again. "Unlikely. I mean, who would she be hiding from?"

Tasha pursed her lips. "You're right, it doesn't look good."

Ed came running to meet them as they parked the car next to his cabin.

"Any sign?" Yvonne asked as she got out.

"No, nothing." He ran a hand through unkempt hair.

"Ed, why didn't you report her missing straight away? And why didn't Matt say something? We spoke to him yesterday. He didn't say a word."

He hung his head.

"You're playing with fire, considering what's been happening to members of your community. Why keep something this important from us?"

"We didn't report it straight away, because we were breaking the law. Pheasant shooting should be as illegal as fox hunting. Not that the law takes the fox hunting ban as seriously as it should, but our intention was to release pheasants which were the property of Ryde Hall. We could all face prosecution for that. Besides, we hoped that Eva had given up and gone home."

Yvonne shook her head. "It's been two days, Ed. Her family reported it to us after you reported it to them. There are questions you need to answer, but for now we'd like you to take us to the last place you saw Eva. We have teams headed to Ryde Hall as we speak. They'll be checking the outbuildings and talking to Emmanuel Tunicliffe, but I'd like to get an idea of where she was, in case she never made it that far."

"Fair enough." Ed nodded. "If you drive, I'll take you to where we were before we split up."

On the way to Ryde, Yvonne continued to question Ed. "Why did you split up? Why did you and Matt separate from Eva?"

Ed sighed. "I didn't want us to split up. I felt it needed all three of us to liberate the pheasants. But Eva said that if Matt and I created a diversion, far enough away from the poultry, it would buy her time to get the pheasants out. The staff have shotguns at that place and CCTV monitoring the yard. She didn't think we could free the birds any other way. To be honest, I thought the whole mission was risky, and I wasn't sure how many pheasants we would save. But Eva couldn't bear the thought of them being in those cages and wearing those masks to stop them pecking each other to death out of stress. You know, the females can't get away from the mating males. And even after they survive all that, they sell them on to other estates for the shooting season. Eva wanted to be the difference."

Yvonne pressed her lips together, able to identify with Eva's sentiments, but unable to comment on them.

Matt gave them directions, until they reached the roadway at the edge of the wood. Yvonne parked the car, and they continued on foot, climbing over the stile and into the adjacent field.

"This way." Matt pointed.

"Wait, Matt." Yvonne placed a hand on his arm. "Don't tread the same path you did that night. Take us around it. We want to avoid interfering with any traces of Eva. Show us where she was and I'll get forensics out here."

"You see that tree?" He pointed to a large oak at the edge of the wood. "That's where we split up. She followed the track through those trees, to the back of the Ryde outbuildings. We saw her start on that pathway and we carried on around."

Yvonne nodded and took out her mobile. Relieved that she had two bars worth of signal, she phoned Dewi.

29

CORRUPTION

The following day, the team gathered for the morning briefing, with Eva still missing. SOCO found several prints that could have been from her trainers. If they belonged to Eva, it suggested she had spent some time in hiding. SOCO were still working the ground, and the team waited on tenterhooks for further news. In the meantime, Dewi had dug up some dirt on Futurecon, Bannerman Holdings and a corrupt council official and was about to fill the team in.

"What you got, Dewi?" Yvonne called, trying to get above the muffled voices in the room.

Her DS cleared his throat and scribbled on the whiteboard. "I don't know if this is related to the murders, but Jake Bannerman of Bannerman Holdings and Serena Wells of Futurecon had a public row just over three months ago. It made all the local news channels and several national newspapers. Both companies attempted to buy officials on the local council to get land rights and planning permissions. The council struck a councillor off and he's facing prosecution for taking monies from both parties. Bannerman and

Wells each believed they would be favourite to have the land near Llanidloes and rowed about it in front of protestors. Neither admitted at the time that they had paid a councillor to influence the board."

"Wow." Yvonne scratched her head. "Somehow, it doesn't surprise me that Bannerman tried underhand tactics, but Serena Wells? I'm a little surprised at her. Do we have the name of the councillor they bribed?"

Dewi nodded. "That's a matter of public record, ma'am. His name is Evan Jones, and they suspended him pending trial. It's certain, however, that his council career is over."

"I see." Yvonne pursed her lips. "How does this relate to our case? And will it help us find Eva Wilde?"

"Apparently, it was environmental protestors who found out about the shady dealing. They suspected councillor Jones of wheeler-dealing and had a friend of theirs hack the councillor's emails."

"Wow, a motive for revenge, right there. Do you think councillor Jones is involved in the deaths?"

Dewi shook his head. "Unlikely. Or, if he is, he got someone else to do it. He was in custody when Krysta was murdered, facing further, unrelated charges of corruption."

"Wow. Good work, Dewi."

"Thanks, ma'am."

∽

TASHA JOINED them for the briefing. The DCI, having agreed in principle to her consultancy, had had it signed off by the superintendent.

Yvonne was so happy about this, she had to fight the urge to smile, on and off, all morning, believing her team would assume she had lost the plot and was not taking the case seriously. This could not have been further from the truth.

As she made a cuppa, the intrusive smile returned.

"What's with the big grin?" Tasha was at her shoulder. "Are you okay?"

"Tasha." A flush moved up the DI's face. "No. I'm not okay. Listen, whilst you're here, I am sorry about tea yesterday," she said, referring to their missed meeting at the tearooms.

"Hey, it's no biggie. The case must take priority, I know that."

Yvonne nodded. "Do you want a coffee?"

"That would be great, thanks. So, why are you not okay? Surely, it's not about our missed date?"

Yvonne shook her head. "When I get a chance, I will talk to you. I can't here."

"You're being enormously cryptic, Yvonne. It's not like you." Tasha laughed and shrugged her shoulders. "Whatever. How's your suspect list coming on? Any favourites?"

"Yes. Two in particular, Tunicliffe and Bannerman" She filled the psychologist in on why they topped the list.

"Can you bring them in for formal questioning? I could take a look at them."

Yvonne shook her head. "Not yet. We need evidence. I also need to speak to Evan Jones."

"The councillor?"

"Ex-councillor, yes. I feel like we've got all the pieces of a complex jigsaw and we're not placing them in quite the right place. Eva is still missing. We need a breakthrough, and we need it, now. As soon as Dewi is ready, we'll go see Evan Jones and Serena Wells, again."

30

ISOLATION

As Eva impacted ground, pain rippled through her like an electric shock.

Her captor didn't speak, but she heard him grunting and felt the wind in her face. She knew she was somewhere in the open, but only the faintest hint of light got through the blindfold. Under her, the earth had the barest stubble of grass, like she was on a moor where the sheep had grazed the land to within an inch of its vegetative life.

Her abductor was cutting the rope, painfully twisting her wrists in the process. As the knife chafed the threads, she readied herself to fight.

She needn't have bothered. As her hands fell loose, he struck her to the side of the head. It gave her tinnitus and took the fight right out of her. There was no resistance as he wrapped her arms around the tree, palms outward, and drove a square-headed nail through them and into the trunk.

The young woman screamed in agony, like she would never stop screaming, though the gag in her mouth prevented it from reaching the full blood-curdling level such pain deserved. Tears streamed down her face as she begged him to stop.

"Please, please, you don't have to do this."

The muffled plea made no difference to the man's actions. He continued tying a rope around her upper arms to prevent her from tearing her hands free.

As he stretched out her tied legs in front of her, she shook with a violence only a body in severe distress can do, wetting herself in the process. He tied her thighs together so that there would be no movement of her legs. Then he left her alone, the warm wind clawing at her body like a barbed whip. The noise from his vehicle faded to nothing.

31

TIGHTROPE

Ed came into the station to enquire about Eva.

Yvonne took him into an interview room.

"Well? Have you heard anything?" His voice had a strangled quality, as though he wanted to cry and was holding back. His forehead shone in the light from the overhead lamp.

"No. Not yet, Ed. I'm sorry."

"What are you doing to find her?"

"We've got teams scouring the wood where she was last seen, and volunteers from the public out looking in other places of interest. We're doing our best."

He grunted, running his hands through his hair.

"In the meantime," Yvonne continued, "tell me about the email hack you guys carried out on Councillor Evan Jones."

Ed flicked his eyes up to hers. "You think it has something to do with her disappearance? Is it connected?" There was a desperation in the wide-eyed look he gave her.

"Honestly? I don't know, Ed. But I would like to know everything you know and which you have not, so far, been telling me. We can't help you if you won't help us."

"Well, yeah, we hacked the councillor's emails. We felt it was the only way that we could show everyone what the hell was going on. We knew there was some sort of dodgy dealing going on, but had no way to prove it. So, we planned and carried out the hack."

"Who was the hacker, Ed?"

"Eva."

"What?"

"Eva." He repeated.

"Eva Wilde?"

A frown furrowed Ed's face. "What's the matter? You think she wouldn't be capable? She is a skilled programmer. She built our website. We're not the mud-eating, tree-dwelling, technology-hating creatures you think we are." Ed spat the words.

"I didn't think that, not for one minute." Yvonne only just kept on a level, herself. "I just wasn't expecting you to tell me it was Eva. That's all. It's not that I wouldn't think her capable."

"But you expected it to be a guy, didn't you? You of all people. A female DI."

She had to admit that he was right. She had thought the hacker would be a male and now felt ashamed of that fact. "You're right. I was expecting you to give me a man's name, and that was anachronistic of me. I'm sorry." She meant it. "Who knew that Eva was your hacker?"

"Nobody."

"Really? You're sure of that?"

"Yes. We never divulged the source, though we may have to at the councillor's trial. Wait, do you think he's involved? Do you think these attacks could be some sort of revenge?"

"He was in custody when Krysta was murdered." Yvonne

Angel of Death

refrained from saying anything further, aware that Dai was looking into the ex-councillor and his connections and she planned on interviewing Evan Jones later that day.

"Hmm." Ed rubbed his chin.

"I've got to go now, Ed, but I will keep you informed. We are doing everything in our power to find Eva."

Ed got up. "If we don't find her soon..." His voiced tailed off.

Yvonne nodded. "I know."

∼

EVAN JONES HAD A WASHED-OUT PALLOR, save for the red nose and cheeks which suggested he might be a spirit drinker. He looked older than his fifty years and his nose bore two deep indents from his glasses. He regarded her with disdain.

"Thank you for coming in to see us, Mr Jones. I know you have had a busy time with police and courts in recent months and I realise that this is likely adding to your stress."

He inhaled deeply before replying. "Well, they say that once you come onto police radar, you are always under scrutiny, don't they?"

"I've no idea. It's not true, in any case." Yvonne sighed. "I've asked you here to enquire about your whereabouts last Friday night, and in the early hours of Saturday morning." She was referring to the night Eva Wilde went missing, though she did not want to specify that.

"I was at the local, sinking several pints."

"Where's your local, Mr Jones?"

"The Red Lion. I live in Berriew village." He frowned, as though she should know that the Red Lion was his local.

"Can anyone verify your presence at the pub?"

"Ooh, let me see... Only about ten people including the landlord." He grinned at her, but there was no warmth in it.

"I see."

"Can I go now?"

"What can you tell me about the hack of your emails?"

"Nothing. I'm facing trial for corruption. You know that. Anything I say could prejudice my case."

"Do you know who perpetrated the hack?"

He shook his head. "Only that it was a bunch of environmental protestors. Why? Do you know who did it?"

"I'm asking you the questions, Mr Jones." Yvonne sat back in her chair. "When does your trial begin?"

"August."

"Do you know anything about the murders of Krysta Whyte, Terry Lloyd, Robert Griffiths and Sarah Jones?"

"There you go." He hissed air through his teeth. "A bunch of protestors hack my emails and get me accused of corruption, and I murder a pile of them just to get my own back because that's what I would do, wouldn't anyone?" He sneered at her.

"There's no need to take that tone, Mr Jones."

"Stop calling me Mr Jones. My name is Evan."

"Evan."

He sighed, taking her by surprise. His voice became softer. "Look, whatever else I may or may not have done, I'm not a killer. I don't have a violent bone in my body. Whatever anger I felt against the people who hacked my email account, it would never have spilled into anything physical. Ask anyone who knows me. I drink more than I should and take anti-depressants like they're smarties. I never go out, except to the pub. I shop online. I don't hurt people or want anyone else to hurt people. I want my life back. So, I'll answer the questions I have to, and I'll do whatever penance is meted out to me. Then I'll try to get a semblance of normal life back. That's it. Take it or leave it."

Her instincts told her he was sincere. It was enough to convince her she should look elsewhere.

∼

DAI CAME RUNNING down the stairs to greet her as she finished in interview room one.

"Ma'am, Serena Wells is on the phone for you."

"Right. Thanks, Dai."

Yvonne took the stairs two at a time, before getting her breath back and picking up the call. "DI Giles."

"Hello. It's Serena Wells, CEO of Futurecon. I understand you wanted to speak with me. Sorry I cannot come to the station. I'm on my way to Paris for an energy conference. What did you want to speak to me about?"

"I wanted to ask you about the public spat you had with Jake Bannerman and the attempts to bribe councillors for land permissions."

Seconds passed.

"It's business, Inspector. It happens. Jake Bannerman got annoyed because he assumed he would get the rights. He saw himself as the only one ruthless enough to get the upper hand. I beat him to the rights. Did he tell you that?"

"I haven't spoken to him about it, yet. I wanted to ask you if you identified the individual who hacked your emails to Evan Jones and what you did when you found out that your private communications had become public."

"I was angry. What more can I say? I wasn't given the name of the hacker, if I had, I'd have given them a piece of my mind."

"Did you learn anything at all about the hack?"

"Well, only that it comprised a team of environmentalists. To be honest, this sort of thing is par for the course in business. There is always someone trying to get inside information. If it's not protestors, it's rival companies. At first, I suspected Jake Bannerman as being behind the hack."

"Really?"

"Yes, until I found out that his emails had also fallen victim, and contained material far more incriminating than mine."

"Did they?"

"I'm no saint, Inspector Giles. I do what I need to, to survive. There are things I've done which do not make me proud, but I try to be as ethical as I can and I don't set out to hurt or mislead anyone. The money I offered to councillors was supposed to speed up the land deals, not make them happen. The faster these things move, the less expensive they end up. That saving can be passed to consumers."

"And increase dividends to shareholders."

"That, too."

"Ms Wells, as you will be aware, four protestors were murdered, and another is missing. Have you or anyone in your security team seen the missing woman?"

"Eva Wilde?"

"Yes."

"Only on the Welsh news on the BBC."

"We are concerned about her welfare."

"If it helps, I am, too, though I am not impressed with the scores of people wandering all over our sites looking for her."

"The public are trying to help and, on our own, we can't spare the manpower to search large swathes of Mid-Wales."

"I just hope they do no damage, Inspector, as I suspect you wouldn't be up for paying for it if they did."

Yvonne sighed. "Eva could be in real danger. If you hear anything, please get in touch."

"I will."

"Thank you." Yvonne clicked the phone down, her head banging. Why was everything always so difficult?

32

TIME RUNNING OUT

Eva's head lolled forward as sleep threatened to overtake her. She'd been fighting it, feeling that to give in to sleep would be to give up on life. She had tried calling out to someone. Anyone. But her gag and the wind made the whole effort futile, even if there had been a person able to respond. She didn't know where she was and wished her would-be killer had at least taken the blindfold off.

She wondered how long it had been since he had nailed her to the tree, but pain and sporadic consciousness made time a nebulous entity. The light seeping through her blindfold suggested it was still daylight, the only thing she could be sure of.

Although not hungry, she had a raging thirst. When fever took over, she thought he had returned and was pouring water into her mouth, even felt it going down. As the fever abated, she realised in distress, there was no water and her thirst was worse than ever.

For the first time she considered the real possibility she would die. Not that she hadn't thought she might before, but this time she considered dying without a coexisting hope that someone would find her. She knew she was somewhere remote. She hadn't heard a single vehicle since he left. No sounds at all, in fact, save the wind in the trees.

Eva thought of Yvonne Giles, the tenacious Inspector she had spoken to in the days before her would-be killer abducted her. She pinned her hope to the image of that police officer. As she fell asleep, it was Inspector Giles Eva was seeing.

~

"YVONNE, THEY'VE FOUND THE MALLET!" Dewi came running in and grabbed hold of her arm. "The search team on Tunicliffe's land found a mallet, hidden under a fallen tree in a stream close to where Eva was last seen."

The DI's eyes flicked from side-to-side as she contemplated this new development. "Right, let's get it checked for prints. If this is our killer's weapon, we get his prints, we get him."

"SOCO are on it, ma'am. They're expediting the results and we should hear as soon as they get an answer."

"Great. Have uniform go to Ryde Hall and keep an eye on Emmanuel Tunnicliffe. If SOCO don't get anything from the mallet, we should still interrogate him and his gamekeeper, Tindall."

"Right."

An hour later, and SOCO were on the phone. They identified the only prints found on the mallet as Eva Wilde's. The killer, if the mallet were his, had worn gloves.

"Well, it's disappointing." Yvonne sighed. "But, at least we know that Eva held the mallet. What if she had somehow grappled it from the killer and hid it so he couldn't use it on her?"

"It's plausible." Dewi nodded. "In that case, what happened to her? And where is she? Is she hiding out?"

"Is the search ongoing down there?"

"It is."

"Good. She may still be in that wood. I want Ryde Hall and it's outbuildings searched. I'll get the DCI to request an urgent warrant. The fact they found a mallet on Ryde Hall land with Eva's prints all over it, should be enough. Also, check with Ed, in case Eva took the mallet with her. If she did, I would still want a search of Ryde Hall conducted, we'll just know that mallet is not the killer's. We'll need to know if DNA is found on the mallet head, too."

"On it, ma'am."

∼

"Tasha, what you said about the killer watching his victims die..." Yvonne ran her hands through her hair.

"What are you thinking?"

"That, if Eva has fallen prey to the Angel of Death, he'll want to watch her die. I'm thinking we could follow Tunicliffe and Tindall. See where they go. If one or both of them is responsible, and we arrest them on suspicion, Eva could pass away before we ever find out where she is."

"What if she's dead already?" Tasha frowned.

"A possibility, I agree, but with no corpse discovered yet, I am hoping she's still alive. Dewi and Callum can tail Tunicliffe, while we locate and follow his gamekeeper, Tindall. What do you say?"

"Will we have backup?"

The DI nodded. "I'll speak to the DCI about permission

to have a team on standby. The helicopter, too, in case we have a casualty in need of urgent medical help. By now, uniformed search officers will be working their way through Ryde Hall outbuildings. Eva might be in one of them."

Tasha nodded. "We can't discount that she may have had an accident and is lying somewhere in the sheds."

~

DEWI MET her at the gates of Ryde. "Tunicliffe isn't here, and neither is his gamekeeper."

"Really?"

Dewi put his hands on his hips. "The search of the buildings is well underway, they're using bolt cutters to open some of the sheds."

"Locked?"

"Yes, probably to keep burglars out, but, who knows?"

"Is Tunicliffe's Land Rover here?"

"No, ma'am."

"All right, we'll head down to Tindall's place, anyway. It's just possible Tunicliffe is there. Can you follow us down when you're ready?"

"Will do."

Yvonne headed back to Tasha, who was waiting for her next to the car. "Come on, we're going to-"

"Yvonne?" Dewi came running out of the gates towards her.

"What is it?"

"They've found a pot in one shed that looks like someone has used it for making home-made glue."

"Rabbit glue?"

"Possible."

"Tasha, a change of plan. Let's go investigate. Dewi, are

SOCO here?"

"No, ma'am."

"Can you request them ASAP and have them get a sample of the glue to the lab as soon as?"

"Will do."

"Clear all non-essential personnel from the shed, until SOCO arrive."

"Okay, will do. Oh, one more thing, ma'am, the DCI is on his way."

Yvonne pulled her mobile from her pocket. Two missed calls from Llewellyn. "Okay, Fine. Tell him we've gone to Tindall's cottage."

∼

TINDALL WASN'T HOME, and neither was his pickup. Yvonne pursed her lips, hands clasped together on the top of her head. "Damn."

"What do we do now? Go looking for him?"

"We must. If that pot held rabbit glue, then either Tunicliffe or Tindall is our man. Who knows, maybe they are both involved? Either way, Eva needs us. While there is hope, we can't stop."

"How close are we to where Eva was last seen?" Tasha's eyes skimmed the surrounding trees.

"They found the mallet with her finger prints about a quarter of a mile that way," Yvonne said, pointing in the direction leading from behind the house.

Tasha rubbed her forehead. "If I'm right, and the killer likes to watch his victim's die, he'll have taken her to a place with little chance of being disturbed. There are police all over. He wouldn't risk being stopped with an incapacitated girl in his vehicle, so it will be close."

Yvonne considered this. "You're right. Let me see, there's a place, up at the Kerry Ridgeway, near to here and above the place where we found Krysta's body. When we attended that scene, we left the police vans in a dirt area next to a gate. There was a big yellow sign telling the public to keep out. I saw the name of a utility company on the sign. I remember it was a water company. It's remote up there. The boundary of Tunicliffe's land is somewhere along that ridge."

"Shall we go have a look?"

"Let's do it," Yvonne called, running back to the car whilst checking her cuffs and mace were in her pocket.

∽

Eva woke to find that she had thrown up all over herself. She heaved and turned her head to vomit again. The sound of a vehicle in the distance ignited hope in her. She stretched her neck as far as she could, trying to get the driver's attention. As it grew closer, she recognised the throaty, diesel engine and that small spark of energy dissipated as fast as it was generated. My God, he was coming back.

The engine died, and the door opened and shut. Heavy boots strode towards her, before he ripped off her blindfold. The light blinded her, her eyes blinking, trying to focus as they streamed from the dust in the wind.

Towering above her, head tilted, he surveyed his handiwork. In his right hand, he twirled a feather between his fingers in front of her face.

"You." She spat the word, shaking her head. Her tongue sticking to the roof of her mouth. She took a moment to free it. "I should have known it was you." She didn't want to look at him anymore. She knew why he was here. He was here to finish it.

"This is my place. You and your kind come camping out here, throwing your weight around. You don't care that we are doing the same things as we've done for centuries. Well, I'm not one of your new men. I don't cry and I don't hug trees. I work this land, the way it's been worked since the beginning of time. If I need to kill or maim, I do it. It's nature's rules."

"Psychopath," she muttered under her breath.

"That's not very nice, is it?" He pulled her head back by the hair, the fingers of his stiff leather glove chafing her scalp.

"You're sick. You need help." Her voice took on a softer tone as though to calm him.

"You lot lack manners, do-"

The sound of a car in the distance stopped him in his tracks. He let her go, stilling to listen. The car had stopped just short of their position.

Eva strained to see, it sounded like the vehicle was just below where they were, about a thousand yards away. She held her breath, her head stinging where he had pulled her hair.

"They're coming for you," she hissed at him.

He struck the side of her head. "Quiet."

His chest heaved as he pulled a knife out of his pocket, crouching to press it against her throat.

"Not a sound." He rasped, as his free hand once more gripped her head by the hair. He turned, as though he expected someone to arrive at any moment.

Whoever it was in the car, they had not yet broken the horizon.

33

SHOWDOWN

As they closed the car doors, Tasha came around to join the DI. "Okay, what now?" she asked in a low voice.

"We find a place where we can look without being seen. We're fine behind this hedge, but if the killer is there and sees us first, we're in trouble."

"Fine. There's a gate just along there."

"Great. Keep low."

They made their way along the hedgeline to a metal gate and crouched. Tasha stayed behind Yvonne as the DI inched her face forward enough to get a view.

"Anything?"

"No. I can't see anyone. On the other side of the field there's another hedge, and trees beyond that. We should stay low and make our way to that second hedge."

"No problem. I'll be right behind you."

The field was dry, well-grazed and littered with black nuggets of sheep dung. Neither Yvonne nor Tasha cared.

As they reached the hedge they heard voices. The DI

turned to Tasha with a finger to her lips, whilst signalling with the other hand to keep low.

They listened but there was no further sound. They crept along the hedgeline until the DI found a hole large enough to give her a view.

She put a hand to her mouth.

"Are they there?" Tasha whispered.

"Yes. Jesus, it looks like Trevor Tindall. He's got Eva."

"Is she alive?"

"I'm not sure. Wait, I'll call for backup. She'll need medical treatment, if she is and we'll need help."

Tasha took over observing through the gap in the hedge, while Yvonne called it in.

When the DI finished, her screen displayed a call from the DCI.

"Hello, Chris?"

"Where are you? What's happening?"

"We are up on the Kerry Ridgeway, We've found Eva. Trevor Tindall is with her and it looks like she is up against a tree. I'm not certain she is alive, but I think I may have heard her speak. I hope I'm right. We are looking at them through a hole in a hedge." She gave the DCI the same directions she had given when requesting backup.

"Hold tight," he ordered. "Do nothing until your backup and I arrive. Got that?"

"Got it, sir."

"Good. I'll be with you as soon as I can. We'll have lights but no sirens."

Yvonne ended the call and rejoined Tasha. "What's Tindall doing?"

"He knows we're here."

"What?"

"Well, he doesn't know we are here, but I'm sure he

heard the car. He's acting furtive and looking around. Eva is alive. I saw her head move. She's not in good shape, though. We need to end this now."

"I know. The cavalry is on the way. Llewelyn ordered me to sit tight." She pursed her lips.

Tasha placed a hand on her shoulder. "I'm not sure we've got that long."

The DI chewed the inside of her cheek. "How would we get to them without his seeing us? How close does this hedge go?"

Tasha pointed to their right, speaking in a low voice. "I think we could go around the outside of the field, that way. Follow the hedge until we get to the field in front of the treeline. If we can get to the trees that side, without being seen, we could come around the back without him spotting us."

Yvonne nodded. "Could work. What if he sees us?"

"You've got your mace and cuffs?"

"Yes."

"Taser?"

"No."

"Better not be seen, then."

"Are we going to jump him?"

"We have to. Otherwise, he could kill her before the teams are ready to move."

Yvonne took a deep breath. "Let's do it. I'll lead. I'm the one with the mace and cuffs."

She set off down the hedgerow, bent almost to a crouch, she moved as fast as that posture would allow, holding her breath as they picked over dirt and stone.

Tasha followed close behind.

It took two minutes to get down the side of the field to where another hedge ran perpendicular to theirs.

"How do we get past this?" Tasha whispered, looking

along its length for a way through. "We can't roll over the top, he'll see us."

"There." Yvonne pointed to a gate twenty yards further on. "We can climb between the bars."

"Good. Let's go."

With reaching the trees, came the most difficult part of their journey and a greater chance of being seen.

Yvonne put a hand out to stay Tasha. "What's he saying to her?" she whispered.

"I can't make it out." Tasha pointed. "I could try and get an arm around his neck. Do you think you can mace and cuff him, when I get hands on?"

Yvonne shook her head. "I can't let you do that. I'll grab him."

"But I can't do mace or cuffs." Tasha grimaced. "And we have to go in, now."

"Fine, but please be careful."

"I'll move to that tree over there, then make a run for it. I will signal you just before I go, for you to follow me with the mace, okay?"

"I'll be right behind you."

As soon as Tindall had his back to them they made their move.

All Yvonne could feel was her heart thudding in her chest. She prayed this wouldn't turn into a panic attack. She couldn't let Tasha down, not now.

What happened next, did so in slow motion. Tasha leapt onto Tindall's back, her forearm pressing hard into his throat.

He growled and grunted and the DI tumbled, as she moved in close enough to spray him in the face. What should have been two short bursts of mace, became a prolonged squirting in the face, as Tasha clung on, preventing him from getting a swing at her with his knife and coughing as she, herself, was caught in the spray.

He bent over double, spluttering and swinging the dagger around in the air, looking to rip open anything that came into its path.

Yvonne moved in to grip the knife arm, twisting it at the elbow and wrist, to take him to ground.

Tasha jumped off and helped.

With the DI's knee in Tindall's back, they managed to get the rigid cuffs on him and Yvonne kept him face-down in the dirt, while Tasha ran to Eva.

After placing under arrest on suspicion of kidnap and attempted murder, Yvonne turned his head to the side, so he could speak.

"Why?" She asked.

"You wouldn't understand." The words were grunted and laden with disdain.

"Try me."

He said nothing further, even as two uniformed officers grabbed his arms and hoisted him off the ground to take him away. But, if expressions could kill, Yvonne would have joined the other victims.

∼

BY THE TIME the DCI and the rest of Yvonne's team had joined them, three marked cars and two vans were in position alongside two ambulances. The dog team had not yet arrived.

The DCI peered down the road. "Where are they?" He spoke into his handset to the leader of the armed response team, to check they were in position.

Dr. Rainer, the trained negotiator, arrived with a loudhailer. One of the armed officers ushered her to the DCI. They could hear a helicopter approaching in the distance.

The DCI held his hand up to stop Dr. Rainer. "Wait a minute, I'm not sure what's happening. My DI said she'd wait here and there's no sign of her."

A call came over the handsets.

It was Yvonne, asking for immediate medical help for Eva, as she struggled to keep Tindall under control.

Tasha untied Eva's legs and supported her arms to prevent further tears to the flesh of her palms.

"He hated us for caring." Eva sobbed.

"I don't think it was as personal as that." Tasha shook her head. "There is so much more to what he did. He has deep psychological problems, that meant that he would have killed, anyway. If not environmentalists, then some other group. It was as much your availability to him as it was your beliefs. You were out and about on his patch, when others were not. If you hadn't been, he'd probably have been driving around looking for other victims, such as those out alone, late at night."

Tasha squeezed Eva's shoulder as the medical teams and other officers took over. "You were so brave, Eva. You're a survivor. We'll check on you, later."

Tasha straightened up and winced in pain. Yvonne ran to her. "You're bleeding." She pointed to Tasha's left side, and a bloodied tear in her blouse.

"Oh, wow." Tasha lifted the material. "I thought I'd kept his knife away from me, but I guess he must have caught me, anyway. It's nothing major, just a scratch. I didn't feel him do it."

"Let me see," Yvonne ordered, bending to examine the wound. "You're right, you were very lucky, it's not too deep.

You're coming with me. The paramedics can check you over."

34

REVELATION

Yvonne arrived at the cottage at around six-thirty, a little later than she intended, having followed a trailer for the last third of her journey. She hoped she hadn't spoiled whatever Tasha was preparing for dinner, not that she could eat much. The shivering in her stomach would make eating difficult. It was time to let out everything she had buried deep within, to be honest with herself and the person she loved more than anyone in the world.

As she entered through the front door, the smell of cooking hit her and she inhaled with a smile, heading for the lounge. Instead of the psychologist, she found the sliding doors wide open and ran through them to the dunes.

Standing atop the sandy mounds, she scoured the beach for Tasha and saw her dark form near the sea. She jogged towards her.

The sound of the waves prevented the psychologist from hearing Yvonne's feet on the sand or her heavy breathing as she ran. Yvonne slowed to a walk and caught her breath, coming up behind her friend whose wistful gaze was still out to sea.

She warmed her hands by rubbing them on her sides, before placing them over the psychologist's eyes. "Surprise!"

Tasha swung round, a grin lighting her face. "There you are. I worried that you had changed your mind."

"What?" Yvonne laughed. "Never." She tilted her head, her face sobering. Her heart skipping beats as the sun glinted off Tasha's chocolate hair, and sparkled in her dark eyes, just like it danced on the sea. She placed her hands on the psychologist's arms, her gaze flicking around Tasha's face.

"What? What is it?" Tasha asked, her brow furrowed, eyes holding tremulous questions, fragile as birds.

"You have never looked so beautiful."

Colour rose along the psychologist's neck, spreading into her cheeks. "Oh, stop it." She smiled, looking at her feet.

"I mean it." Yvonne put a hand underneath Tasha's chin, raising it to look into her eyes. "There's something I've been longing to tell you. Something burning a hole in me for weeks. I have to tell you now, or I swear I will spontaneously combust."

Tasha searched her face. "Then tell me," she whispered, her expression paused between sorrow and ecstasy.

"I love you." Yvonne's gaze was steady. Sure of itself. "I don't know why it has taken me so long to admit it to myself, much less why I never admitted it to you. But, I love you. I love you. I love you. I don't want to be with anyone else."

Tasha looked at her, open-mouthed, unsure if what was happening was real or created by her own imagination, wanting it for so long.

"Am I too late?" Doubt invaded the DI. Her hands trembled.

"Oh, Yvonne." Tasha pulled her into her arms. "You're shaking."

"So are you."

"I adore you, don't you see that?" Tasha put a hand each side of the DI's face. "I thought this moment would never come. I thought I would only ever be your friend. I rebooted my life to be near you. To be where you are. Did you not realise?"

Yvonne wasn't sure who started it, but their lips met and the kiss took over, deep, passionate and unfettered.

Everything that had been wrong, was right. Everything confused, made sense, the way nothing had since she lost her husband all those years ago.

As they walked, arms around each other, back to the cottage, happiness uplifted every part of the DI. The future invited her with open arms and she was finally ready to walk into it.

ALSO BY ANNA-MARIE MORGAN

Book 1 - Death Master

Book 2 - You Will Die

Book 3 - Total Wipeout

Book 4 - Deep Cut

Book 5 - The Pusher

Book 6 - Gone

Book 7 - Bone Dancer

Book 8 - Blood Lost

Book 9 - Angel of Death

AFTERWORD

If you enjoyed this book, I'd be very grateful if you'd post a short review on Amazon. Your support really does make a difference and helps bring my books to more readers like you.

Mailing list: You can join my emailing list here : AnnamarieMorgan.com
Facebook page: AnnamarieMorganAuthor

You might also like to read the other books in the series:
Book 1: Death Master:
After months of mental and physical therapy, Yvonne Giles, an Oxford DI, is back at work and that's just how she likes it. So when she's asked to hunt the serial killer responsible for taking apart young women, the DI jumps at the chance but hides the fact she is suffering debilitating flashbacks. She is told to work with Tasha Phillips, an in-her-face, criminal psychologist. The DI is not enamoured with the idea. Tasha has a lot to prove. Yvonne has a lot to get over. A tentative link with a 20 year-old cold case brings

them closer to the truth but events then take a horrifyingly personal turn.

Book 2: You Will Die

After apprehending an Oxford Serial Killer, and almost losing her life in the process, DI Yvonne Giles has left England for a quieter life in rural Wales.Her peace is shattered when she is asked to hunt a priest-killing psychopath, who taunts the police with messages inscribed on the corpses.Yvonne requests the help of Dr. Tasha Phillips, a psychologist and friend, to aid in the hunt. But the killer is one step ahead and the ultimatum, he sets them, could leave everyone devastated.

Book 3: Total Wipeout

A whole family is wiped out with a shotgun. At first glance, it's an open-and-shut case. The dad did it, then killed himself. The deaths follow at least two similar family wipeouts – attributed to the financial crash.

So why doesn't that sit right with Detective Inspector Yvonne Giles? And why has a rape occurred in the area, in the weeks preceding each family's demise? Her seniors do not believe there are questions to answer. DI Giles must therefore risk everything, in a high-stakes investigation ofa mysterious masonic ring and players in high finance.

Can she find the answers, before the next innocent family is wiped out?

Book 4: Deep Cut

In a tiny hamlet in North Wales, a female recruit is murdered whilst on Christmas home leave. Detective Inspector Yvonne Giles is asked to cut short her own leave, to investigate. Why was the young soldier killed? And is her death related to several alleged suicides at her army base? DI Giles this it is, and that someone powerful has a dark secret they will do anything to hide.

Book 5: The Pusher

Young men are turning up dead on the banks of the River Severn. Some of them have been missing for days or even weeks. The only thing the police can be sure of, is that the men have drowned. Rumours abound that a mythical serial killer has turned his attention from the Manchester canal to the waterways of Mid-Wales. And now one of CID's own is missing. A brand new recruit with everything to live for. DI Giles must find him before it's too late.

Book 6: Gone

Children are going missing. They are not heard from again until sinister requests for cryptocurrency go viral. The public must pay or the children die. For lead detective Yvonne Giles, the case is complicated enough. And then the unthinkable happens...

Book 7: Bone Dancer

A serial killer is murdering women, threading their bones back together, and leaving them for police to find. Detective Inspector Yvonne Giles must find him before more innocent victims die. Problem is, the killer wants her and will do anything he can to get her. Unaware that she, herself, is is a target, DI Giles risks everything to catch him.

Book 8: Blood Lost

A young man comes home to find his whole family missing. Half-eaten breakfasts and blood spatter on the lounge wall are the only clues to what happened...

Book 9: Angel of Death

He is watching. Biding his time. Preparing himself for a torturous kill. Soaring above; lord of all. His journey, direct through the lives of the unsuspecting.

The Angel of Death is nigh.

The peace of the Mid-Wales countryside is shattered, when a female eco-warrior is found crucified in a public wood. At first, it would appear a simple case of finding which of the woman's enemies had had her killed. But DI Yvonne Giles has no idea how bad things are going to get. As the body count rises, she will need all of her instincts, and the skills of those closest to her, to stop the murderous rampage of the Angel of Death.

Book 10: Death in the Air

Several fatal air collisions have occurred within a few months in rural Wales. According to the local Air Accidents Investigation Branch (AAIB) inspector, it's a coincidence. Clusters happen. Except, this cluster is different. DI Yvonne Giles suspects it when she hears some of the witness statements but, when an AAIB inspector is found dead under a bridge, she knows it.

Something is way off. Yvonne is determined to get to the bottom of the mystery, but exactly how far down the treacherous rabbit hole is she prepared to go?

Book 11: Death in the Mist

The morning after a viscous sea-mist covers the seaside town of Aberystwyth, a young student lies brutalised within one hundred yards of the castle ruins.

DI Yvonne Giles' reputation precedes her. Having successfully captured more serial killers than some detectives have caught colds, she is seconded to head the murder investigation team, and hunt down the young woman's killer.

What she doesn't know, is this is only the beginning...

Book 12: Death under Hypnosis

When the secretive and mysterious Sheila Winters approaches Yvonne Giles and tells her that she murdered someone thirty years before, she has the DI's immediate attention.

Things get even more strange when Sheila states:

She doesn't know who.

She doesn't know where.

She doesn't know why.

Book 13: Fatal Turn

A seasoned hiker goes missing from the Dolfor Moors after recording a social media video describing a narrow cave he intends to explore. A tragic accident? Nothing to see here, until a team of cavers disappear on a coastal potholing expedition, setting off a string of events that has DI Giles tearing her hair out. What, or who is the thread that ties this series of disappearances together?

A serial killer, thriller murder-mystery set in Wales.

Book 14: The Edinburgh Murders

A newly retired detective from the Met is murdered in a murky alley in Edinburgh, a sinister calling card left with the body.

The dead man had been a close friend of psychologist Tasha Phillips, giving her her first gig with the Met decades before.

Tasha begs DI Yvonne Giles to aid the Scottish police in solving the case.

In unfamiliar territory, and with a ruthless killer haunting the streets, the DI plunges herself into one of the darkest, most terrifying cases of her career. Who exactly is The Poet?

Remember to watch out for Book 15, coming soon...

Printed in Great Britain
by Amazon